ANTONIO CANALES

**Also by Travis Myers
&
Natasha Myers Marsiguerra**

Sister Margaret

Hayden Jon Marshall

Jenny Black

Li Jun

A Fairly Violent Life

Sol Abramowitz

William Tell

Praise for the Detective Tommy Keane series:

"Detective Tommy Keane is one true-blue streetwise cop. But what makes him exceptional is his honest soul. That's a combination that can keep you turning the pages deep into the night."
- Jay Schadler, 20/20, ABC News, Nightline, Good Morning America, and National Geographic.

"From the streets of the Bronx to the Upper East Side, Sister Margaret offers a tantalizing glimpse of NYC crime where nothing is ever what it seems, and fighting it is anything but routine."
- NYPD Police Commissioner, Dermot Shea.

"Devious, intense, and disturbing."

-Zoe Williams, whatsbetterthanbooks.com Best Book Blog 2017.

"You can't get any more New York than Detective Tommy Keane. Reading this series is like walking in the shoes, and seeing through the eyes of a man who embodies the city, nail-biting, shocking, and fascinating, these stories are the real deal - and highly addictive."

-Meg MacCary, Desperately Seeking the 80's Podcast.

"A gut punch of a tale that takes the reader behind the crime scene tape and onto an exhilarating tour of the streets, drug dens, dive bars, and precinct houses of New York City, with an

insider's view that rarely makes the papers."
- Jesse Smith, Crime Journalist, Kingston Times.

"The Myers Siblings create real, raw, heart-wrenching crime fiction like no one else in this genre."
– Kayla Waters, True Crime Exposed Podcast.

Tommy Keane is the man! Travis and Natasha write their books in a way that makes it easy to follow yet gives you great detail and keeps you wanting more! They are absolutely my favorite crime authors of all time!
- Sam Sprunger, The 500 Section Lounge Podcast.

"NYPD Detective Travis Myers spent years "on the job" in the Bronx. Now, Travis and his sister Natasha bring to life the escapades of fictional detective Tommy Keane in these fast-paced police procedurals."
- Peabody Award-Winning Investigative Reporter, Host of the True Crime Reporter Podcast, Robert Riggs.

"Authentic and engaging crime fiction."
    – Sandra Mangan, crimefictionlover.com

"An exciting and interesting read, loaded with plot twists, consider me an official Tommy Keane fan!"
– Suzie Que, Punkoleum Magazine.

ANTONIO CANALES

A Tommy Keane Novel

Travis Myers &
Natasha Myers Marsiguerra

Published in the United States by Bully Press Corp.

Bully Press Corp
P. O. Box 404
Wingdale, NY 12594 United States
www.bullypress.net

Cover design by: Phred Rawles

ISBN-13: 979-8-9890119-8-8

For The Lost Boys

***

Dedicated to every Cop and Detective, in every city, in every country on the planet. Thank you for standing on the side of right, and for fighting the good and never-ending fight against those who would destroy all we hold dear.

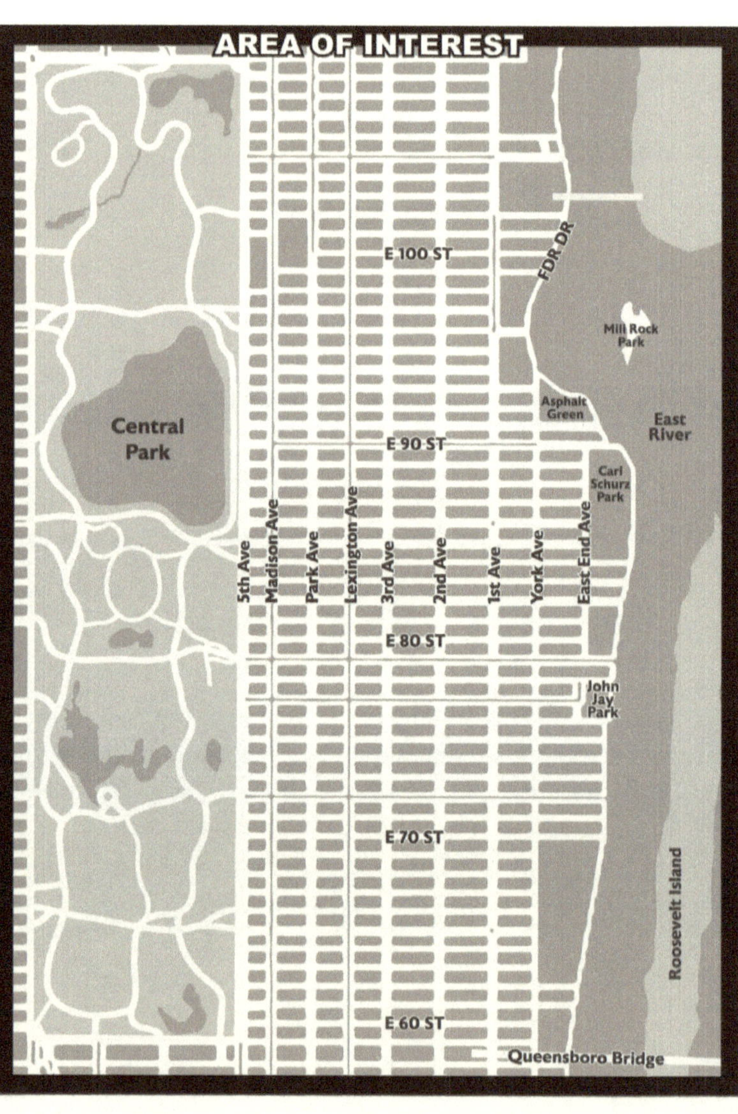

AREA OF INTEREST
Central Park
E 100 ST
E 90 ST
E 80 ST
E 70 ST
E 60 ST
5th Ave
Madison Ave
Park Ave
Lexington Ave
3rd Ave
2nd Ave
1st Ave
York Ave
East End Ave
FDR DR
Mill Rock Park
Asphalt Green
East River
Carl Schurz Park
John Jay Park
Roosevelt Island
Queensboro Bridge

"Senseless violence is a prerogative of youth, which has much energy but little talent for the constructive."

-Anthony Burgess, A Clockwork Orange.

Prologue

Tommy was thirteen years old the first time someone he had known was violently killed, an older boy of sixteen who lived a block away from the building Tommy grew up in, named Steven, a poor kid with an absentee father, a drunk for a mother, and no future to speak of.

Steven had nothing and needed everything, so desperation got the better of him one morning. He decided a quick and easy robbery would help him make it through the week. He took a navy blue knit watch cap and cut two slits in it where his eyes would be, turning the hat into a makeshift balaclava.

He then took an old, broken plastic cap gun from his younger brother's toy box, wrapped the handle in black electrical tape, removed the bright orange tip from the barrel, and patched up any imperfections with a black magic marker. 'I'll be in and out of there in a flash,' he thought to himself. 'They'll never realize it's only a toy, and I'll be gone.'

Steven made his way over to the River-X RX Pharmacy on York Avenue. He pulled his homemade mask down over his face, took the little modified cap gun from his pocket, and entered the store. He demanded that the girl, twenty-year-old Lara Stern, empty the register into a paper bag for him. Once she did, he turned, and as he placed his hand on the doors push bar, "Bang!" one deafening shot rang out.

The pharmacist and owner of the business, William Loersch, who watched the robbery take place from behind the Rx counter, stepped out and let a single round go from his legally registered .38 special revolver. It caused both he and Lara Stern to jump in shock from the weapon's loud boom, and young Steven to collapse dead in the doorway, with a gunshot wound to his head.

Steven wasn't a friend of Tommy, but he was a kid from Yorkville, someone like so many others, whom you know enough to nod to and say, "What's up, Steven," when passing on the sidewalk or meeting in a pizzeria.

But something about Steven's death rang true to Tommy, Terry, and the rest of their little friend group, who predominantly hung out on 89th Street. That a violent death was no longer a thing of stories from the older guys in the neighborhood, or some gangster movie on TV, it happened to Steven, and sure, he may have put himself there, but it happened, nonetheless.

A year later, a young man of seventeen from the same housing project Terry lived in, named Eric Brown, died. He had a long-running beef with a crew of older kids who hung around the projects and were known as the Towers Gang or the Towers Boys. He made the deadly mistake of throwing a piece of a broken brick at three of the Towers Boys in retribution for a beating he had taken from them in the past.

The brick missed its intended target, but unfortunately, found the shoulder of a seventy-two-year-old aunt of one of the gang's members who had left for the military some months before. The young men, Joey Raft, eighteen, Kenny O'Dell, seventeen, and Augustus (Gusty) Cole, fifteen, chased Eric Brown into the front of one of the Holmes Towers.

Eric hit the elevator button feverishly but knowing it would never make it down in time, he took the stairs, hoping to make it to his fourth-floor apartment unscathed. He did not.

The three youths caught him on the steps between the third and fourth floors and beat him to death. Fists, feet, and knees pummeled young Eric until he went limp, then the boys picked him up and threw his body down the concrete stairwell as one last act of vengeance against the thrown brick.

All were arrested. Joey and Kenny both pleaded guilty to manslaughter and were put away. Joey, the eldest, served 5½ years, and Kenny received 3 years. The youngest, Gusty, also took a plea and received 11 months at the Spafford Juvenile Center in the Bronx, NY. The first of many arrests and convictions he would face in the years to come.

By the time Tommy and Terry were seventeen, there were other names of friends and acquaintances added to the list of lost boys. Teenagers destroyed by violence, and or drugs. A list that was punctuated when Terry himself, while being attacked in the bathroom of Julia

Richman High School by members of the Cigar Mob Gang, stabbed one of his attackers to death.

It resulted in his incarceration for three plus years in the infamous Sing Sing Correctional facility in Ossining, New York, and Tommy dropping out of high school and joining the Army's 82nd Airborne to serve as a paratrooper.

***

Over the years, Tommy and Terry realized and came to accept the fact that there was an unavoidable thread of violence that ran through every New Yorker's life. This thread wasn't bound only to poorer street kids; it was one that even wealthy prep school kids knew existed. There was that hesitation to walk down an unfamiliar street or fear when stepping into an empty subway car alone, where the safety-in-numbers rule was absent.

Once violence became apparent to boys like Tommy Keane and Terry Calahan, it would not only be a reality that they would learn to deal with and harden themselves against but also turn into a tool to be used.

If used well and controlled properly, it would serve them every bit as well in their world as a hammer serves a carpenter, a knife serves a chef, or a lie serves a politician.

Neither man had a violent nature, though both learned to befriend violence and use it when needed to bring an end to any number of situations. For men like Tommy and

Terry, violence could be turned on and off as quickly as the flick of a light switch; it was, for the most part, a passionless tool to be pulled from the box and employed whenever deemed necessary.

Chapter One

Delmonico's Italian Steakhouse. Albany, New York.

Tommy sat across from his beautiful nineteen-year-old daughter, Caitlyn, who meant the world to him, at Delmonico's Italian Steakhouse. It was a little after 9:00 PM on a Saturday, and Tommy had taken a well-earned week off after the William Tell case to drive up to visit Caitlyn at Sienna College and spend some much-needed quality time with her.

It was almost May, and he hadn't physically seen Caitlyn since her Christmas break. Between the demands of her college life and the ridiculous hours he put in at work, the few phone calls and text messages they shared weren't enough to satisfy either of their relationship needs.

Tommy's vacation was going well. He relaxed during the first couple of days of his week off, which he spent in his very quiet White Plains apartment. He had gotten plenty of sleep, his diet and exercise routine were back in order and on track, and, in true Tommy Keane fashion, he had been able to relatively swiftly come to terms with, and purge many of the horrors and stresses of the William Tell case out of his being.

He was far from a new man, as every grim case would leave yet another scar and another ghost, in this circumstance, several ghosts. But Tommy, well, he had a gift few have for resilience. After his first three days off, he was about 99% himself and ready to take a trip to visit his favorite person on the planet —his sweet little girl, Caitlyn.

Tommy drove up from his mother's place on 88th Street the night before. He treated Caitlyn and her boyfriend, Nick, to Nick's favorite area restaurant, a Chinese chain called PF Chang's, but this Saturday was Father/Daughter Day. They started with a simple lunch at the Lathem 76 Diner and then headed over to the Colonie Center Mall. He spoiled her with a half-day shopping spree, during which she bought several new outfits, a pair of boots, and a pair of sneakers.

The two talked for hours. They discussed Caitlyn's classes and professors, her growing relationship with her boyfriend, something Caitlyn was delighted her dad was receptive to and seemed happy about. Tommy's ex-wife— Caitlyn's mother, Cookie.

Although Tommy still very much loved his ex-wife, Cookie, he wanted more than anything for her to be happy and content with her life. From everything he had heard about Cookie's current relationship, it seemed like it was nothing but favorable. Her new love interest, Michael, was a respectable, hardworking widower who owned his own insurance business and did well for himself and his two sons.

However, when Caitlyn asked about Tommy's life, he was less forthcoming. Caitlyn had seen a lot about the William

Tell case and also had questions about Li Jun and the Hayden Jon Marshall cases, as well as all of his police work in general.

Now that she was a grown woman and learning more and more about the world, a curiosity grew in her. Before, her father's job was no more than an abstract idea; he was a cop who arrested bad people, and that was it.

But now, as she matured, she realized there was a lot more to her father and the life he had led not only for the last nineteen years of her life but also for the twenty-seven years prior to her birth.

But in true Tommy fashion, he deflected her questions, changed the subject, and, on occasion, answered with, "You don't want to hear about that," or "I don't want to tell you about that."

When pressed on his love life, a topic Caitlyn was definitely interested in after seeing Molly, the unbelievably beautiful woman who was only six to seven years her senior, basically wrap herself around her father while he lie in his hospital bed, in front of a dozen other people the morning after he had been shot in the head during the Li Jun case, well, Caitlyn wanted to know, and wanted to know everything there was.

But Tommy almost shyly answered with a simple, "She's just a girl I know from the neighborhood," and something like, "Nothing serious there," which of course piqued Caitlyn's curiosity.

Caitlyn had always adored her father, looking up to him as some kind of hero. But it was in the way a child looks up to a father, or family member, and she was beginning to realize that there was a complex and sophisticated man in her presence, with a complete and mysterious life full of adventures, stories, loves, dangers, and many things she had never thought of, 'Who is this man? My father, who is he really?' she thought to herself as she watched him speak to her in his calm way. 'Will I ever know?'

The waitress, a young blonde college girl, saw that Tommy was done with his steak and asked Caitlyn if she was finished with her half-eaten chicken piccata.

"Yes, thank you," Caitlyn responded. The waitress took her plate and asked if they were interested in any dessert.

"Hell, yeah, I am, I'm on vacation this week!" was Tommy's reply.

"Very good, sir, I'll be right back."

Tommy looked at Caitlyn, a meaningful look deep into her eyes, and with a half-one-sided grin said, "I love you, kid. I'm extremely happy I made it up here this weekend."

This took Caitlyn back a little. Her father told her he loved her whenever he saw her, or they spoke on the phone. This time, however, his looking into her eyes the way he was and feeling it was coming from somewhere deep, hit her a little hard. As she replied, "I love you too, Daddy," she could feel a tear welling up in her eye.

Tommy could see something emotional brewing behind Caitlyn's eyes, so he leaned back slightly and looked around the restaurant—the brick archways, the oak trim, the black and white checkered tablecloths. "Charming place, isn't it?" he said, turning the conversation to mundane small talk.

"Yes, yes, it's a beautiful spot," she smiled.

The waitress returned with a dessert cart loaded with cakes, pies, and Italian pastries. "See anything you like?" she asked.

Caitlyn ordered a cannoli and a cappuccino, and Tommy a slice of amaretto cheesecake and another unsweetened iced tea.

As the conversation resumed, Tommy's phone began to buzz. Not recognizing the number, he answered, "Keane here."

"Tommy… It's Terry. I need your help. The cops … detectives from your precinct picked up our Shane a little while ago. They're saying he done a murder down in Carl Schurz Park, saying he killed some kid by bashing his head in with a Belgian Block. We know he had nothin' to do with this, but they got him, scooped him up at his apartment like maybe two-three hours ago. Are you working? Do you know anything about this?"

"No, no. I'm away at the moment, visiting Caitlyn. I don't know anything about this. Please tell me more; tell me what's going on."

"What I told you is really all I got. A couple of detectives went by his place and grabbed him up They're charging him with the murder of another boy from the neighborhood named Tony. The kid was found beaten to death with a big Belgian Block, you know, a cobblestone crushing his skull over by the Peter Pan statue in the park. Supposedly, it's a really bad scene."

"Fuck me, what do you know about Shane's whereabouts at the time?"

"All I know is he was home when he got picked up; don't know what time Tony was killed… I don't know Tony, but from what I understand he was a great kid, well liked in the neighborhood, but I'm tellin ya Tommy, I'm fuckin tellin ya, no way Shane woulda done this, no way in the world."

"I believe that Terry, I don't know Shane well, but he certainly doesn't seem to be a kid who would do something as savage as you described, now listen to me, I'm about three hours away, let me make some phone calls to see what I can find out, then I'll head right down there okay, I don't know, but figure maybe four hours or so I should arrive at the precinct, or on scene… And what's Shane's last name?"

"Thanks, Tom. We're in a spot here, and?" Terry paused for a second, surprised. "His last name is Southerland."

"Southerland? Is he one of our Southerland's?"

"Yeah… he's Queenie's boy."

"Fuck me, I didn't know that, how the? Why the fuck didn't you ever mention that?

"I figured you knew. Why would I have to mention it?

"Oh wow, this is a surprise… Queenie's boy, wow, I had no idea. I can see it now."

"Yeah, maybe you been out of touch with the neighborhood a little too long there, Tommy. Shane is Queenie's boy."

***

Queenie Southerland was a dear friend of both Tommy and Terry from their teenage years. She grew up in a tumultuous family with a drunken bum magnet for a mother, who let her girls run around the streets fending for themselves as if they were feral dogs.

Her elder sister, Fiona, became a drug-addicted prostitute in her teens, and as a pre-teen, Queenie became the head of her household, making sure her younger sister Amy (Amelia) and the rest of the family ate and that the bills were paid.

As an adult, Queenie, along with Terry Calahan's tutelage, and help from the neighborhood's infamous Devine brothers, grew into one of the most well-known and dangerous shylocks (money lender – loan sharks) in New York City. Queenie was a shrewd and ruthless businesswoman who no longer had any problem paying her rent or keeping the lights on.

Queenie wasn't sure who Shane's father was and, therefore, had one of the finest men she knew, her lifelong friend, the arch-criminal Terry Calahan, act as young Shane's father figure.

Shane, who had just turned thirteen, may as well have been Terry's natural-born son, as he was almost a carbon copy of the man who ran the streets of the small enclave of Yorkville north of 86th Street.

Terry taught Shane everything he knew about the world, and Shane, who, like his mother, was quite bright, devoured every bit of information handed down to him. Between his mother, Queenie, and his father figure/mentor and hero, Terry Calahan, Shane was being fast-tracked into the life of New York City's criminal underworld. A life most mothers would dread their children's involvement in, but Queenie instead groomed her son for it.

She knew this life was inevitable, given her and her family's circumstances. To her way of thinking, if Shane were in this life, he would be prepared for it. She wanted her son to live as a lion in this world of thieves, not as a sheep.

***

Tommy took a breath, "Okay, I'm gonna get on the phone and see what I can find out, then get in the car and head down there, tell Queenie, I'm on my way… and also, tell her not to mention my name, I want my inquiries to go smoothly, and I don't want this to appear like I'm involved or there's a conflict of interest, at least any more than I'm going to have to let on."

"Right, you wanna control the narrative."

"Something like that, yeah… Alright, I'm gonna hang up, and I'll keep you posted."

"Thanks, brother. Talk soon."

Tommy hung up the phone and then stared down at his cheesecake for a moment.

"What happened? That didn't sound good at all." Caitlyn asked.

"Just – just a little neighborhood trouble I need to look into. Looks like we're going to get some boxes for these desserts. Does your Nick like cheesecake?"

"Are you kidding me?" Caitlin responded in the affirmative, but then asked, "Are you sure everything is alright, Daddy? You look worried."

"No, everything is fine, dear, nothing for you to worry about."

Tommy took Caitlyn back to her dorm, hugged and kissed her goodbye, and then returned to his little Honda CRV, where he sat for a bit and then called the squad.

"2-1 Squad, PAA Tate speaking. How may I help you?" Charice Tate answered the phone.

"Hey, Charice, how you doing, love? It's me, Tommy."

"Detective Keane, you handsome man, you calling Charice from vacation cause you miss her so much?"

"Of course I am, Charice, you know a week without Charice is like a week without sunshine! But I also want to ask about a homicide, case of a boy killed in Carl Schurz Park?"

"Oooh, honey, that was a bad one. It happened two nights ago. They got the kid, though; a little baby-faced demon did it."

"Who caught it? Who made the arrest?"

"Detective Stein caught that one. He and Clay and Doreen scooped him up a few hours ago; I think he may be off to Horizons by now."

"Okay, thanks, Charice. I'll get with Stein on his cell; have a good night, dear."

"You too, Tommy, enjoy the rest of your vacation!"

Tommy immediately called Mark Stein.

"Hey, Tom, how are you?"

"Eh, I've been better, Mark. I'm calling you about a kid you picked up earlier today, Shane Southerland."

"Yeah, we grabbed him like five hours ago on his way home, killed another boy over in the park, Carl Schurz Park, over by the statue of Peter Pan; you know where that's at?"

"Sure, I do, (a memory flashed of the first time Tommy kissed Rebecca Rivera in front of that statue when he was fifteen.) What's the story there?"

"This Tony Canales was beaten to death with sticks or bats and had his head crushed in with a hefty Belgium block. Absolutely awful injury. I don't have much. It sounds like this Shane and some friends did it, but this Shane is as close-mouthed as they come. I haven't gotten a word out of him. Only thirteen, but already he's a rough customer; why? Why are you calling?"

"I heard about it. I wanted to get the story straight. A little bird told me you got the wrong kid, so I wanted to give you a call and see what's up."

"Oh, really? Pretty sure we got the right one; he was no help to himself, and neither was his mother, but we got a witness putting him in the park, and word is he was the ringleader, that he and his friends jumped this Tony kid over a past dispute, and the dead boy actually wrote Shane on the pavement in his own blood."

"Wow, so you have a witness plus his name in blood; that doesn't sound favorable, and what does he have to say about it?"

"Nothing really, kept telling me, 'You made a mistake,' and 'You got the wrong guy.' That kind of stuff."

"And the mother, you said she was difficult too?"

"Not so much difficult, but taxing to deal with. I don't know if you're familiar with the name Queenie Southerland. Super fierce lady, from up around the projects, she's a known associate of the Calahan crew from the Holmes Towers on 92nd Street, anyway, she was extremely closed mouth, like her boy, showed up with a lawyer, they wanted him released, but with the severity of the crime that wasn't going to happen, not to mention her record."

"So, you still processing him?"

"No, Clay and Doreen took him up to Horizon (Horizon Juvenile Detention). Sounds like you're interested in this kid; everything alright?"

"Well, yeah, yeah, I am, he's a decent kid; I know him from the Hayden Jon Marshall case; he was the one who found and fingered the building where all those kids were being held."

"No shit? Well, he's off to Horizon now, and to be honest with what we have, I don't think we could have done anything to keep him out of there; right now, he's our number one, and this was a very horrific scene."

"It's bad, huh?"

"Bad."

"Listen, I'm on my way down from Albany. I don't want to be jumping into one of your cases, but if you don't mind, I'd like to take a look at what you got, I, I mean, fuck me, Mark, I don't know this kid well, but I don't see it, I just can't see it being him."

"No problem, Tommy, please come on down and take a look. Listen, everything we have says it is, but we've all been wrong before. Come on by, take a look, and tell me what you think. I've only started putting this case together… Hell, if you have some kind of relationship, maybe you can get this kid to talk, even give up who he was with."

***

Tommy pulled onto the block where the precinct stood. It was almost 1:00 AM. He found parking around the corner, quickly walked back to the 2-1, and rushed up the stairs, hoping Mark was still in the house. He was.

"Hey, there you go," Mark said as he saw Tommy enter the room, "I finished up a little bit ago and have to head down to the courthouse tomorrow, but I wanted to wait and see if you showed."

"Yes, sir. I got down here as fast as I could and got lucky with a spot around the corner, so yeah, please let me see what you got."

Mark reached across his desk with his case folder, the name Antonio Canales written on the top in black magic marker. Tommy took it, sat across from Mark at Doreen's desk, and opened it.

"Oh man!" Tommy turned his head slightly and grimaced in reaction to what he saw, "You weren't kidding when you said it was bad," Tommy exclaimed as he looked at the crime scene photos. One Antonio Canales, a young man of fifteen, had a large grey granite Belgium block sitting inside his skull where the back of his head should be. Blood and brain tissue were forced out around the area that the heavy stone had crushed. "My god, this is awful." He continued as he flipped through each of the photos.

Tommy then stood up, spread out all the pictures on the two adjoining desks, and studied them for a moment.

"I, I see where he wrote his name, where
he wrote Shane here, in his own blood." He commented in a
low voice.

"Yeah," Mark replied, "Doesn't ring true to you?"

Tommy looked back up at Mark. The way he said it, he
knew it didn't ring true to him either.

"No, not really."

"I have my doubts as well, but go ahead, tell me why?"

"Well, if this kid is taking an active beating, he's not
going to be able to write, right? I mean, who can write while
you're being beaten? You're either going to cover up, or you're
going to run, or you're going to fight back. I can't see
this kid writing the name Shane as he waits for his skull to be
crushed like this. I'm not saying it's not possible,
just seems unlikely."

"I agree, certainly possible, but unlikely, because he
couldn't have done it after he was hit with the block that killed
him, and it seems to me his attackers would have cleaned or
smudged the name before or after they dropped the block on
his head."

"Any other weapons recovered?"

"Yes, we had a short child's baseball bat and a fourteen-
inch end of a mop handle; both had blood, but no prints were
recovered."

"I see you got a couple of footprints."

"Yes, two decent ones, the front half of
a size eight sneaker."

"And our boy Shane?"

"Size eight."

"Tell me about the witness."

"Two, actually, young neighborhood girls were walking
on East End and saw four boys running out of the park at
86th Street; they say the only one they recognized was Shane,
knew him by name from school."

"So, they go to school together, where?"

"Wagner Junior High, they say this Shane kid barely
attends for whatever that's worth."

"These are the interviews?" Tommy picked up two
pieces of paper, each containing a statement, one from an Iyana
Franco and the other from a Stephanie McCrain. "Kind
of scant, girls didn't have much to say?"

"No, not more than they saw Shane, who they both
knew from school, and three older boys running from the
park."

"And you just locked him up like, what, eight hours
ago?"

"Yeah, about five o'clock, we got his address and sat
and waited for maybe an hour and a half, and he came walking
down the block, and we grabbed him. Little fucker was so hard,
he never shed a tear, never got excited, and he wouldn't

even give us his mother's number; we had to get a hold of her on our own."

Tommy smirked a little and thought, 'Yeah, he's a true Yorkville boy,' then looking up again at Mark, "Wouldn't even give you his mother's number, huh?"

"Nope, it was like having a mini James Cagney in the chair, and his mother, fuckin hell is she a severe piece of work, came in with a lawyer beside her, but she spoke right up and told the kid outright to keep his mouth shut, said they'd find out what was going on and that he would have to be locked up for a few days, told him to take no shit while he was inside, and the woman never shed a tear."

"She give you a hard time?"

"No, not at all; like I said, she was rough, looked like she wanted to rip my face off, and she was particularly direct, only told me once that I had the wrong kid, but rude, uncivil? No, not at all. To be honest, it made her a little scarier; she was serious business."

"So, you got to meet with the ADA tomorrow on this, right?"

"Yeah, first thing in the morning."

"Alright, thanks for waiting for me and letting me look through everything, Mark. I hate to keep you."

"Please, don't worry about it. I appreciate your insight, and besides, I haven't signed out yet, so I'm still doing the almighty overtime."

"Ha, good man, listen, I'm still off until Wednesday, but I may join you in court tomorrow if that's cool with you?"

"Yeah, sure, that's fine, Tom; you genuinely have an interest in this kid, don't you?'

"Well, yeah, I kinda owe him… I'll see you tomorrow, pal."

"Goodnight, Tom."

\- 24 -

Chapter Two

Tommy left the Squad room and, on his way out of the precinct, called the number where he had received Terry Calahan's call hours before.

"Hey Tommy, how you doing?"

"Doing alright, I got to the city a little less than an hour ago, and got with the guy who caught the case, unfortunately, Shane is already up at Horizon by now, but after seeing what I saw and knowing what I know about this case, there would have been no way to keep him out of the system, this was an unbelievably vicious attack on this kid, and currently the little evidence we have points directly at Shane."

"Well, we know it wasn't him; I'm telling you that right now, Tommy!"

"And I believe you, and I believe it myself. Listen, where are you? I'd like to do this in person rather than on the phone."

"I'm at home with Sissy and Queenie… Go to Reif's, we'll meet you there."

"Very good, I'm on my way, be about fifteen minutes."

They both hung up.

2:12 AM Reif's Tavern 302 East 92nd Street.

Tommy parked at the fire hydrant close to Reif's and headed inside. As he did, he took in the scene: Terry stood at the corner of the bar, his wife Sissy, seated closely next to Queenie, who also sat at the bar, and Anne Marie, who stood directly behind the two women with her arms draped around them both.

There were no tears, but a solemn air in the room, even among the unknowing patrons drinking and partying throughout the rest of the small bar. Tommy felt as though he was entering a funeral home for a wake rather than a pub on a Saturday night.

Tommy shook Terry's hand, and they had a quick embrace. He then turned to Queenie, but before any words were exchanged, Anne Marie stepped in between them, gave Tommy a big, tight hug and a kiss on the cheek, and said,

"You're gonna fix this, aren't you, Tommy? You're gonna get our Shaney boy out and back here with his mother where he belongs, right?"

Tommy heard Anne Marie's words, but his eyes were locked on Queenie's. He hadn't seen his dear friend in over a decade, and even then, it was only a quick hello in the street. Tommy was both happy and brokenhearted to see her.

He was happy because, as he did Terry, he sorely missed her. He was brokenhearted because of the reason for their meeting and knowing the unbelievable pain she must have been going through with her thirteen-year-old son sitting in a correctional facility in the Bronx, and not knowing if he would ever return home.

As Anne Marie embraced Tommy and his eyes fell deep into Queenie's, he was instantly reconnected. He could tell she was with him, too. It was only a moment, but for that moment, the closeness and bond of a cherished childhood friendship was resealed.

Queenie slowly rose from her barstool, her face expressionless, as it was her way never to reveal her emotions, though her eyes couldn't help but show a desperation to Tommy that most would never notice. She hugged Tommy tightly, then pulled back slightly from the embrace, placed her well-manicured hands on his cheeks, and, staring deep into his eyes, said, "Tommy Keane, I have missed you so much." Then, she softly kissed him, "Do you think you can help my boy, Shane, Tommy? Can you bring him back to me?"

"I'm going to do my best, Queens," he paused, fighting off the emotions that the reunion and the circumstances were bringing up. I work with the detective who caught the case. He's a stand-up guy, and I just had a meeting with him. I will be going to court with him tomorrow to see what we can do and where the investigation is heading."

"Yeah, I know about Stein. He's a tough old prick, but it always seemed like he was a fair guy from what I've heard?"

"Very fair."

Antonio Canales

Queenie sat back onto her barstool, and then Sissy stood and hugged Tommy, "It's been too long, Tommy; we miss you; we all miss you so much."

This was the first time in over twenty years that these five people had been in the same room together. Unfortunately, it wasn't a celebration of any sort; in a way, it was more like entering a funeral home, as he had thought before. Here, the five of them met as if it were a wake, and it was, as it was the death of whatever childhood Shane may have had left. He was already a tenacious kid, a throwback to a working-class era that had long since passed in this neighborhood. However, there was now no doubt that any childhood or childlike qualities Shane still carried would be forever lost.

Regardless of whether he was found guilty or innocent of the murder of Tony Canales, Shane would forevermore be an adult.

***

Tommy stepped back from his embrace with Sissy and put his arm behind Terry, placing it on the small of his back, again giving him the slightest of hugs. Then, looking at the three women in front of him, he attempted to raise their spirits a bit.

"Yeah, fuck me, it has been way too long. I can't remember when we all sat together like this. I gotta say, you girls are all looking fantastic, though."

And here, although being intentionally kind, he did not lie.

Anne Marie, who always had one of the best figures in the neighborhood, had kept it up. At forty-six, dressed in tight jeans and a snug-fitting cashmere sweater, she still loved to flaunt it. Her bleached blonde hair was pulled back on the sides, full and big on top, and voluminous at the back. It gave her a youthful appearance, one that only upon closer look would reveal the crow's feet and smile lines of an older woman. And even with her broken front tooth, which she had never fixed over the years, she still tended to be one of the best-looking women in the neighborhood, regardless of her age.

Queenie also kept herself together; she was blessed with a natural beauty that required little attention, like all the Southerland sisters. Her smooth, white skin and soft, brown eyes still shone. Her hair, which carried lovely blonde highlights, and French-manicured nails, were kept up with regular trips to the salon. She always looked and dressed her best. As New York City's preeminent female money lender, it was good business to appear successful, and at forty-seven, she could not have looked better.

At forty-four, Sissy was the youngest and the smallest, standing barely five feet two. Her natural red hair was now obviously dyed a more vibrant shade of red to cover the greys that were rapidly appearing. It had an attractive cut —long and layered —and flowed down around her shoulders, with a slight pompadour in the front, its color further accentuating her bright green eyes. She was dressed in a lovely velour tracksuit, which had become almost a uniform to the neighborhood's now lessening working-class women. Something that wasn't noticed by most, but undeniably a tribal signal to those who belonged.

***

After they all smiled and thanked Tommy for his kind words, Terry spoke up,

"Sissy, Anne Marie, you two beat it to the back. We need to talk."

And both Sissy and Anne Marie did precisely as they were told and immediately left Tommy, Terry, and Queenie to discuss the situation.

Terry then leaned over to a man of about sixty years old, wearing a red plaid Carhartt shirt jacket, who was sitting fairly close to the trio and asked him to get up and move down the bar a bit. The man questioned nothing, knowing who Terry was, and immediately got up, picked up his beer, and made his way further down the bar.

The three of them now sat next to one another, huddled up close on their stools, Queenie beginning,

"Tommy, what do you think you can do? I'm tellin ya, my Shane had nothing to do with this and I'm terrified they're going to put him away for it."

"I'm going to look at it, I'm going to dig deep and do everything I can to find out what happened, but as of right now, like I said, they won't be releasing him, not until something goes in his favor, look, listen to me, Queens, I can't see Shane being involved in this, but, understand this, the little evidence there is, points towards Shane, there are two witnesses who put him close to the scene, and from what I understand he has no alibi," Tommy explained.

"Who are these witnesses?" Terry asked.

"No, no, we're not doing that, Terry; you can't ask about the investigation, alright? In fact, you both are going to be cool, and my name will never be mentioned concerning this or anything else, alright, we can't run the risk of any conflict of interest here. I'm going to do my best to find out what I can and do what I can to uncover the truth, and if Shane is innocent, which I believe he is, because, well, he just has to be… Then he will be vindicated. It may take some time, and it won't be easy for any of us, but I promise to do what I can to help Shane. You got my word on that."

Queenie raised her right hand and placed it on Tommy's cheek as she had before: "I know you will, Tommy. I know you will."

"What are we supposed to do on our end?" Terry asked.

"Just be cool and do what the both of you do best: keep your eyes and ears open. If Shane has nothing to do with this, as we believe, then our thing is to figure out who does, and I don't have to tell either of you, the rumors will be buzzing all over this neighborhood like flies on shit, so pay attention, and note them all, 90% will be bullshit, but," he paused and raised his index finger and his eyebrows to punctuate his statement.

"That other 10% will have a few threads of truth in them, and that's what we're going to have to find - those one or two threads we can pull on to unravel the truth about what happened two nights ago."

Terry and Queenie nodded in agreement as Tommy continued, "But we gotta be cool. If the police or the courts think any of us is interfering in any way, it will go badly for Shane, especially if he's found guilty of having anything to do with this."

"He hasn't! He's had nothing to do with this, I…" Queenie began, but Tommy cut her off.

"I know he didn't, Queens, but us knowing will have nothing to do with what the courts decide."

As Tommy finished, there was a slight commotion from the back of the bar where the pool room was, and Sissy approached quickly and told Terry and the rest.

"Terry! This fucker in the back needs a smack; you wanna straighten him out before Anne Marie does?"

Terry, Tommy, and Queenie straightened up and alerted to the situation: "Does he need to be thrown out or need a smack?"

"He needs a smack. He thought he was being cute, and he slid the pool cue between Anne Marie's legs from behind."

"Oh, really?" Terry replied, and in seconds, Terry and Tommy were in the back, where Anne Marie was still confronting four men in their mid-twenties in the rear room, which held one pool table, a television, and a few high-top tables.

"This mother fucker here! The big one in the Dartmouth shirt!" Anne Marie shouted as her boys entered the room.

The man she was pointing at stood a little over six feet tall, as did two of his friends; the fourth was only about five feet nine inches, the same height as Terry and Tommy. The one Anne Marie was shouting at wore a grey sweatshirt with "Dartmouth Lacrosse" printed on it.

One of the other tall guys had on a blue and white striped dress shirt over a pair of faded blue jeans and flip flops, the other one leaned against one of the tables dressed in a white dress shirt over blue jeans, and the shorter of the four wore a charcoal Nirvana band shirt with yellow print.

All were between twenty-five and twenty-eight years of age, and it was apparent that all had been drinking.

"Step back, Anne Marie," Terry demanded.

The young man in the Dartmouth shirt stepped forward with a pool cue in his hand, which he tapped hard onto the floor as if to make a statement, opened his mouth, and said,

"Whoa, should I be afraid now, you toothless slut? I see you brought your…"

Before another word passed his lips, Terry shot a straight right hand into the Lacrosse player's midsection, and as the man leaned forward from the pain and the shock of the blow, a vicious left hook came out of nowhere, shooting blood across the room onto the wall and knocking the man to the floor.

One of the other young men quickly came from around the side of the pool table to help his friend but was met by a quick over-handed chop to the throat by Tommy, who then swept the man's right leg out from under him, sending him crashing down onto the hard tiled floor of the pool room.

The other two men, the one wearing the white shirt and the other in the Nirvana t-shirt, stood up straight in shock and awe at what they had just witnessed, and both raised their hands, the shorter one saying,

"Yo, yo, yo, they were wrong. We had nothing to do with that!"

The taller one in the white shirt, also with his hands up, concurred with his shorter comrade: "So sorry, so, so sorry. He was, they were definitely out of line."

Terry and Tommy still stood in the doorway exiting the pool room, and as the moment took shape, Terry shouted, "And these two, Anne Marie?"

"Nah, not them, just that motherfucker in the fucking Lacrosse shirt; that was the fresh one; the others did nothing wrong, just that one motherfucker in the grey sweatshirt!"

"You two!" Tommy yelled at the two still standing. Get your two friends out of here before it's too late, you hear me?"

"Yes, yes, sir, right away, s-s-sorry, they were wrong, so sorry," the taller one apologized as the two of them helped their friends to their feet and quickly rushed them out the door. As they passed, Terry slapped the one in the blue and white shirt across the back of the head.

"And don't ever come back here!" he shouted as they approached the front door to exit.

As Tommy and Terry stepped out of the pool room and back into the bar area, Sissy hugged Terry and kissed him.

"Sorry, honey, you didn't need that tonight."

And Anne Marie said, "Thanks, Terry," as she threw her arms around Tommy's neck and gave him a hard kiss on the mouth.

"Woo!" she shouted, "T & T back in the house! Just like old times! Fuck yeah!..." Then, in a reasonable tone, she continued, "Thank you, Tommy, I, I mean we appreciate it, and I, I truly appreciate it."

"It's alright, it's nothing, really."

As they walked back towards the front of the pub, where Queenie sat quietly on the stool she never bothered to get up from. She knew, as cold and ruthless as she was, that violence was a man's business, and she would have only been in the way had she joined them.

Terry pulled a hundred-dollar bill from the wad he held in a rubber band in his pocket and dropped it on the bar.

"Sorry, Phil, you know we didn't want no trouble."

"Of course, Terry, you're never any trouble." Phil, the bartender, replied.

"Alright, let's pack it in; we don't want to be here if these cunts call the cops," said Terry, and all three ladies put their jackets on, and the five of them left the bar, one of the patrons shouting out, "Nice job, boys!" as they left.

As they said their goodbyes, Tommy reassured Queenie and Terry that he was on the job and would constantly be in touch as things progressed.

They all thanked him as they hugged each other good night, and as Tommy began to cross the street, Anne Marie grabbed at his elbow as he turned. He was standing in the street, and Anne Marie was still up on the curb. She kissed him on the mouth again,

"Where you going, Tommy? You need some company?" Dropping her chin, her eyes looking up at him, trying to look as innocent as possible.

"Oh, Anne Marie, you beautiful, sweet thing, nothing would make me happier, but I have to be in court in less than five hours, and I know, oh man do I know, if you were to keep me company tonight, I wouldn't have the strength to make it in, and it's important that I do."

"Tommy fuckin Keane, always the charmer and always such a gentleman; we miss you around here, we really do."

"I miss you too, dear. I miss this neighborhood and how we used to be." He then leaned in and gave her a long, hard kiss; she looked back at him wide-eyed with a full smile, tears of both joy and sorrow welling up in her lovely blue eyes. "Go on, catch up with them, Anne Marie, or I'm gonna have to walk you home, and then I'll never make it to court in the morning."

She headed down the block to catch up with the others, and he crossed the street to his car. As he opened the door and began to enter, he could hear Anne Marie shout, "I love you, Tommy Keane! You are my hero!"

Tommy turned and waved to her as she threw him a kiss.

Chapter Three

9:08 AM

Tommy arrived at Manhattan Criminal Courts on Center Street and, before entering, messaged Stein to see if he had arrived and where he was to go.

"I'm walking over right now. Be there in two minutes. Wait for me, and we'll head up together."

Tommy didn't mind; it was a beautiful morning, and he'd preferred to be outside than in a tiny ADA's office anyway. He leaned against a car and put his face toward the sun. He took a deep breath and let it out slowly. Being at Reif's the night before with his old friends had brought back so many memories. He understood how it had to be now, with their different lives, but he did miss the life they all once shared.

Mark walked down the street and threw his empty coffee cup into the trash can. "Morning, Tom."

"Morning," Tommy replied, "How you doing?"

"Could have used another few hours' sleep, but nothing new about that, I don't think I've had a full eight since I started this job?"

The two detectives entered the building and made their way up to the office of ADA Lidia Schwartz, who had caught the case and had yet to properly review the arrest, although she was quite familiar with the crime that had landed in her lap three days prior.

Lidia was a seasoned prosecutor who had been working homicides for the last four or so years. She was a short, misshapen woman who was remarkably substantial from the waist down but incredibly thin from the waist up. Although almost fifty years of age, she had a charming, childlike quality and smile that made her one of Mark Stein's favorite ADAs in the building.

This would be the third homicide they had worked on together, and both were happy about it. They had mutual respect and admiration for one another's skills and work ethic.

"Good morning, Lidia. It's nice to see you again. This is one of my colleagues, Detective Tommy Keane."

Tommy nodded hello as he put his hand out to shake Lidia's.

"Thee Tommy Keane! Well, hello, Detective Keane, it's truly nice to meet you, sir, I have heard nothing but positive things about you over the years, and I had no idea you were involved in this case, but if it's you and Mark together on this one, I am sure it will be an easy, as they say, slam dunk for me."

"Tommy, please call me Tommy. Technically, I'm on vacation this week and not assigned to this case at all, but, well, I…"

Mark interjected, "Tommy has personal knowledge of our perp, and he doubts his guilt. I am not wholly convinced yet, but there definitely is room for doubt here. It wouldn't be the first time we grabbed the wrong person."

"Interesting. Well, okay then," Lidia said as she walked around her desk and sat. Her office was cramped, filled with file cabinets and bookshelves lining the sidewalls. There were two chairs in front of the desk where Mark and Tommy sat.

She opened her case folder. "Let me ask you right away, Detective Keane. I'm sorry, Tommy. Tell me precisely what your relationship or connection is with this young man." She paused to read his name from the folder, "Shane Southerland. There is, or will be, no conflict of interest between this office, you, Detective, and this alleged perpetrator, will there be?"

"No, no, of course not. My relationship with Shane is basically none, but he acted, or well, became an unofficial CI, or witness, who helped to identify the woman who kidnapped Hayden Jon Marshall. That led us to the building where all those children were being held last Thanksgiving, if you recall?"

"If I recall? Yes, of course, that was such a huge case, and one of the reasons, if I may," Lidia paused, slightly embarrassed at what she was about to say, "I have admired your work so much, Detective, I'm sorry, Tommy…" Lidia took a breath, "Okay then. Well, I can see how you would be interested in checking in and doing what you can for this young man." She paused again, "And you said you're here during your vacation time today?"

"Yes, ma'am, I drove down from upstate last night to be here and to look into this case with you and Mark."

"Where did you come from, if you don't mind me asking?"

"Right outside of Albany, my daughter goes to Siena, and I was spending the weekend with her when I got the news."

"Wow, that's some selfless dedication there; you don't see that often."

"I feel I owe it to the kid, Lidia. If it weren't for him, all those children would still be being held captive."

"You're a solid man, Detective. Okay, give me a minute, gentlemen, while I look this over."

Lidia spent a few minutes reading over the case, the crime details, and what led Mark to make the arrest.

"Well, at first glance, young Mr. Southerland does appear to be our suspect, and under the circumstances of this unbelievably brutal crime, not to mention what we know about his mother's history, there's no way he'll be released at the moment, and where is he? Ah, Horizon, I see, hell of a place for a thirteen-year-old to be."

"I assumed as much, Lidia, but, well, I wanted to meet you and hope to keep your mind open, as is Mark's, that we have the wrong kid here. Honestly, I don't know Shane well, not well at all, but I can honestly say I don't like him as the killer. I've read the report, and Mark and I have discussed the case. Together, we will review every detail to determine whether Shane is guilty. If not, we will do our best to find out who is, and again, personally, I can't see it. I don't think he has this," Tommy reached across Lidia's desk, tapping his fingers hard against the photo of Tony Canales with a granite block where his head should be, "In him… I just can't see it."

"Alright then, we'll still have to go through arraignments, of course, and he will be remanded back to Horizon, but go-ahead gentlemen, please look deeper, and I truly do wish you luck in possibly exonerating this young man, and in bringing whoever is responsible for this horrific act to justice."

During their meeting, Lidia and Mark signed a search warrant for Shane and Queenie's apartment on 90th Street. They planned to search the place later that day, after they returned to the precinct.

***

Tommy and Mark left court and took the subway back to the precinct. On the way, they discussed everything related to the case and decided to ask Lieutenant Bricks to allow Tommy to officially join the investigation.

Once they arrived at the Squad room, they laid everything out on the desk, and Mark again told Tommy what he knew. During the conversation, Tommy observed something that didn't sit quite right with him.

"These footprints, Mark? Something doesn't seem right to me. Now I know you said they proved to be the same size as Shane wears."

"Yes, size eight."

"I'll make a bet with you, Mark; I'll bet we don't find this brand of sneaker, one matching this tread, in Shane's apartment."

Mark paused and cocked his head, very interested to hear why Tommy was willing to make such a bet. "I'm game, but why?"

"You grew up in the city and know how cliquey kids can be. It would have been the same for you and me as for Shane and his friends. Now, what I can tell you is this: the couple of times I have met this kid, he was wearing old-school Adidas Superstars, and something I know is that, for most kids like Shane, his brand will be his brand. I could see him maybe drifting over to a pair of Puma Baskets, or Clydes, but I will bet you we'll find nothing else in his closet, and on that same note, these treads here in this photo, I don't know what they are, but I know what they're not, and that's a pair of Superstars."

"Outstanding observation there, Sherlock, and one that will be noted when we serve the warrant. Do you want to grab lunch and then head over there for that?" Mark asked.

"That sounds good, in case we get mixed up in anything while there and can't eat for hours."

Tommy and Mark headed to 86th and York Avenue and the Mansion Diner for lunch. Both men ordered pastrami Reubens. Tommy got his with mustard rather than Russian dressing, sweet potato fries, and an unsweetened iced tea, and Mark with regular, but well-done fries and a coffee.

Tommy, however, couldn't enjoy his meal. He was a strong man who believed in honor, friendship, and right and wrong. Regardless of how often he would bend rules to the point of breaking, he always believed it was for the greater good.

But here he was eating with his new friend and colleague Mark Stein, about to serve a search warrant on one of his oldest and dearest friends, Queenie Southerland. An act that may ruin this old friendship, jeopardize his new one, and the scariest of all, may put a young man away for many, many years. The whole situation was sickening, and halfway through his meal, Tommy completely lost his appetite.

1:45 PM

Southerland Residence, 315 East 90th Street.

Tommy and Mark arrived at Queenie's building, and Mark rang the bell.

Tommy recognized Queenie's voice. "Who is it?"

"It's the police, ma'am, Detectives from the 21st Precinct." A second passed, and then the buzzer rang, unlocking the door.

Tommy and Mark walked up to the second-floor apartment, and Mark knocked. Tommy stood behind him. The locks began to tumble, and the door opened. Queenie looked at Mark and Tommy with contempt but kept her cool as she greeted them.

"Hello, Stein. How was your night? Better than my son's, I'm sure?"

Stein nodded in recognition of her jab, "Good morning, Miss Southerland. This is my partner, Detective Keane. Here is a search warrant allowing us to search your apartment."

"How you doing, Detective Keane?" Queenie asked with a bit of disgust, "Yeah, come on in and take a look around; you won't find shit cause my Shane didn't do what you're saying he did to that boy." She said as she stepped aside, allowing the detectives to enter.

Queenie and Shane's apartment was a typical old railroad flat common to most of the neighborhood. Mark and Tommy stepped into a nicely renovated eat-in kitchen with black and white mosaic tiled floors, white Carrera marble countertops, and a white subway-tiled backsplash. The walls were all painted white, which contrasted beautifully with the original, refinished, old oak doors and oak wood floors.

"Where does Shane stay, ma'am? We'd like to start there." Mark asked.

"Here, come this way." On the opposite side of the kitchen was a 13 x 11 bedroom with a double closet, two windows covered by iron gates and curtains, a double bed, a dresser, and a desk with a matching wooden chair.

It was surprisingly well kept and clean, and unlike what one may expect to be found on the walls of a thirteen-year-old boy's bedroom, like sports figures, beautiful actresses, models, or Marvel comics characters, Shane had a sizable poster of the Twin Towers at World Trade Center that read 'Never

Forget' commemorating a tragic event that happened years before he was even born.

Over his bed, hung side by side were an English flag and an Irish flag, and above them both was an American flag. There was nothing boyish or childish about Shane's room at all. If one were to guess, you'd think it belonged to a bachelor in his mid-twenties.

"We may be a bit," Mark said as they began.

"I got nowhere to be," Queenie said as she lit a cigarette and watched Mark and Tommy go through her son's things.

Tommy, wanting to prove his point, went straight to the closet and under the bed, looking for footwear, and in doing so, found: one pair of Timberland boots, another pair of black combat styles boots, and a pair of black and brown, dress shoes, and old pair of beat- up white Adidas Superstars with navy stripes, and another pair of red Adidas Superstars with black stripes. Tommy looked up at Queenie from where he knelt next to Shane's bed and asked,

"Are these all of Shane's shoes, ma'am?"

"All but the ones on his feet." She answered, blowing cigarette smoke from her nose as she finished.

"Can you tell me what kind of shoes he would have with him right now?"

"Same Adidas as those dirty white ones there," she said before taking another drag.

Tommy looked over at Mark, who took note of what Queenie had said. Turning one of the sneakers over to show the sole, he said, "See, what I tell you?"

Queenie didn't know what that meant, but it did give her a bit of reassurance. She knew it was a point Tommy wanted to make, and it sounded like a clue that would be in her son's favor.

Mark and Tommy rifled through all of Shane's belongings, into the pockets of every pair of pants, shirt, jacket, and coat. They were respectful and didn't turn the place upside down. In the end, they found nothing but two folding knives, a push-button switchblade, a set of brass knuckles, and two half-full packs of Marlboro cigarettes.

The knives and the brass knuckles were not illegal as they were all inside a residence and not on Shane's person; they did, however, confiscate them to be vouchered and sent to the lab, just in case there was any evidence to be located. They also discovered no drugs or any drug paraphernalia, really nothing incriminating at all, other than the knives and brass knuckles, which, again, were not illegal to possess in one's home, only illegal if carried in public.

Mark and Tommy did a simple, cursory walk through the rest of the apartment, poking their noses into the bathroom, the living room, and Queenie's bedroom, and all the closets, and found nothing to raise their suspicions at all, much to Tommy's relief.

Mark asked Queenie to take a seat, and she complied. They all sat in her living room on her blue tweed sofa set.

"Miss Southerland, I know you believe your son is innocent, and after speaking at length with my partner, Detective Keane, here, and in light of the search we have conducted of your residence, I, too, may doubt his guilt. Now, normally, I would never say that to someone connected to an individual I am investigating, but, well, I am not only the detective who arrested your boy; I am also a father. If possible, I would like you to understand that I have no personal animosity towards your son. My job as a professional is to uncover the truth, nothing but the truth, about what happened in the park a few nights ago. Shane was witnessed at the scene. Other evidence points towards him as well, but in the end, please understand, I don't want your child; I want the truth. Do you understand?"

"I do," she said firmly.

"I will need you to go to Horizon tomorrow so I can re-interview Shane. It was rather challenging to get two words out of him yesterday when I picked him up, as you well know. You were there when I interviewed him, and he was quite the hard case. Hopefully, tomorrow, with your encouragement, he will open up a little.

"Anytime. You tell me when, and I'll be there."

With that, Mark thanked Queenie for her cooperation, and Mark and Tommy left her apartment.

Chapter Four

Tommy and Mark had returned to the Squad room at the 2-1, but Lieutenant Bricks was not in. The entire B team was off that day, except for Mark, who had to attend court for Shane's arrest.

While Mark finished up some paperwork regarding his court visit and the warrant they had served at Queenie's apartment, he and Tommy called him.

"Hey, Lu, how are you? Sorry to bother you today, but I wanted to give you a heads-up about the current status of the Canales case. I presented it all to the ADA, and everything went smoothly. Tommy and I have just returned from the suspect's residence, where we executed a search warrant…"

"Yes, he came down early from upstate. He has an interest in this case; it turns out the kid I arrested is the same kid who tipped Tommy off to the building where those kids were being held during the Marshall case last year…"

"Yes, sir, I will absolutely tell him, yes, Lu. So, we are now having some doubts about yesterday's arrest." I'm going to head back downtown in an hour or so for the kids' arraignment, and I'm going to have Tommy help me out with this case going forward, cool? – Okay, great. Thanks, Lu."

Mark hung up the phone, and as he did, Tommy asked,

"So, what he say?"

"Ha, so first he wants to know why the fuck you're back from vacation, and if you're not on duty, what the fuck is on your mind working?"

"He pissed?"

"No, you know Bricks never loses his temper, but he wants you to write down your hours, and he'll make sure they're taken care of. He's not happy about the liability of you doing the warrant with me without being signed in, but no harm, no foul, and we'll get it all straight."

"Okay, cool, he's a first-rate fucking boss."

"One of the best."

"Alright, Mark, I'll leave you to it."

"Not interested in the arraignment?"

"Nah, I know the kid won't be released. Anyone who sees those photographs will definitely want more than a pound of flesh for this one, plus I'm pretty fucking tired still after last night."

"Alright, my friend. Enjoy what's left of your day. You're back in tomorrow, yes?"

Yes, sir, we'll interview Shane and discuss where we want to take this. What time do you want me in?"

"Let's start at 9:00 AM. I want to make arrangements for Horizon around 10:00 or 11:00."

"Very good. Keep me posted if anything changes. If not, I'll be here at 9:00."

6:22 PM

Tommy opened the door to Brady's Corner Pub; it had been over a week since he had set foot in the bar or seen his dear Molly.

The crowd was thin. No more than a couple of regulars and a few of the after-work crowd sat at the bar; the rest of the room was empty.

Molly, whom Tommy was happy to see, was working the shift as he had expected and hoped, didn't notice Tommy at first, which he appreciated because he loved watching her make her way up and down the bar, charming the old guys and regulars with her fun-loving personality.

Tommy stood at the door, watching her. She was a sight for sore eyes. It may have only been a couple of weeks since the William Tell case had ended, and a little over a week since he had last seen his Molly, but the stress induced on Tommy during the three weeks of that investigation and its immediate aftermath, then his week of decompression where he locked himself in his White Plains apartment for five days and did nothing but eat sleep and go to the gym in an attempt to put himself back together both physically and mentally made it feel more like an eternity since he had felt like his usual self.

Unfortunately, his return was also under worrisome and stressful circumstances. Still, for those few seconds, standing in the doorway of his regular haunt, watching his attractive young girlfriend do her thing behind the bar, keeping her admirers happy and entertained, he felt good, just plain good. Precisely as he did over the weekend, sitting with his darling daughter Caitlyn up in Albany, sometimes all it took was a moment of beauty and of love to remind him that there was positivity in the world and, in fact, that most of the world was indeed decent and not filled with the filth he dealt with daily.

Molly eventually noticed Tommy standing near the doorway, watching her as she washed glasses. She smiled, her white teeth and green eyes glittering at him from the light of a neon sign. She slowly stood up straight from the sink, cocking her head slightly in acknowledgment of Tommy's presence, assuming he had been watching her for a minute, she dried her hands on a bar towel, then rushed from behind the bar and ran up to Tommy, throwing herself into his arms, wrapping her arms around his neck and her legs around his waist; she squealed with excitement.

"I didn't think I'd see you for a few more days!" she said, between the kisses she peppered all over his face and mouth.

"I had to come back early for work." He replied.

"Oh no, you didn't cut your time short with Caitlyn, did you?"

"Yeah, by a day, I'm sorry to say."

"Oh no, I'm sorry, honey. I know you were looking forward to this weekend."

"Yeah, it sucks, but what you gonna do? Crime waits for no man, right?"

"What happened? Why you back? Something bad? That boy in the park?"

"I can't talk about it, Molly, and truly, you don't want to know about it."

"Alright, if that's how you're gonna be, go ahead sit down, sexy man, and let me get back to work and get you something to drink."

Tommy watched this beauty walk back down the bar; her hair still dyed that jet black she had chosen during the William Tell murders. He missed her natural strawberry blonde, but damn if she didn't look great with that
short black hair bouncing around, in her tight blue jeans, and tight red baby-doll t-shirt.

Tommy was not a religious man at all; he had no heaven or hell in his life. But as he watched her turn back in behind the bar and make sure her regulars were all taken care of, he looked up at the ceiling and said softly to himself and the big guy upstairs, "Thank you, God. It's good to know you don't hate me."

An elderly working stiff, sitting next to
the stool Tommy pulled out, asked, "Excuse me, son, I didn't catch what you said."

Tommy looked back at the old man who had one white eye covered over by cataracts and a permanent whiskey grimace on his face that made him look a little like Popeye the Sailor, and replied,

"Na, was nothing Pop, I'm simply glad to be here today," and as he sat in the stool next to him, Molly dropped a coaster onto the bar, followed by a bottle of Bud, a rocks glass to which she poured a double shot of Jameson into for Tommy, and a shot glass to which she poured herself a shot of Shankey's Whip.

"Give my friend here whatever he wants, please, Molly."

Molly gave the older man a shot of Jameson as well, then Tommy raised his glass and said, "To us… Then was joined by the older fella, "And those like us!" and Molly tossed hers back while Tommy and the elderly man took a sip from their glasses.

Tommy smiled. As far as he knew, the only people who knew that toast were from the neighborhood.

"Where are you from, Pop?" Tommy asked.

"Lived here my whole life, originally 83rd off 2nd, now 84th and First, worked 580 (Iron Worker) for thirty-nine and a half years."

"Ooh, long time for that job. I bet you got some stories?"

"Maybe just a million or two?" the old-timer replied. "You spend eighty-one years in a neighborhood like this, you got stories falling out of your pockets."

"Eighty-one? Well, you're looking pretty damn exceptional, sir, if you don't mind me saying?"

"Mind? Shit, that's something I can't hear enough, thank you, son."

Tommy and his new friend chatted about life and Yorkville for about an hour before Molly's shift ended. As they got to know one another, they realized they had a few friends and many acquaintances in common. Tommy bought him another shot and two beers and was deep in conversation when Molly appeared next to them, with her jacket on.

"Okay, Eddie, it's shift change. I'm leaving now with my man here, and it's time for you to go home now, too, honey."

"Your man, huh? Well, it appears you've got a respectable one, Miss Molly. Be as wonderful to him as you are to me, please."

"Tonight, Eddie, I'm going to be way better to him than I've ever been to you." She said with a smile and a wink.

"Ho ho! I know what that means! Good night to you, young bloods, thanks for the drinks and the company, and I, well, I hope to see you again, my friend."

***

Tommy and Molly grabbed a small sausage, black olive, and fresh garlic pizza from Arturo's pizzeria kitty-corner from Brady's. They then walked to Molly's building and made their way up to her apartment. Upon entering, she turned to lock the door, and Tommy placed the pizza on the kitchen counter.

As he turned to face her, she aggressively attacked him, grabbing him by the lapels of his leather coat. She pulled him in close and kissed him hard on the mouth, then forced him to open his mouth with her tongue. She continued to forcefully kiss him until he had to pull his head back.

"Slow down, girl, let me catch a breath," he said, laughing.

"No, no talking you! I haven't seen you in almost two weeks," she said, pulling his jacket down around his elbows. "No words tonight, only action," she continued as she pushed his coat down his arms and onto the floor.

"I like where this is going," Tommy began, but was cut off when she grabbed him by the face and said again, "No, no talking," before kissing him one more time and biting him hard on the lip, "Now, get these fucking clothes off and get in my bed!"

Tommy did as he was told and stripped in the kitchen, with a boyish grin on his face, as Molly quickly rushed towards her bedroom, pulling pieces of clothing off along the way.

It took him a minute to untie his shoes and get naked before making his way to the entrance of her room. He found her laying on her bed, her head and shoulders propped up by pillows, two candles softly lighting the room, their light flickering on her pure white skin, her feet flat on the mattress, her knees bent, and legs spread apart showing every bit of her femininity, Tommy gazed upon this beauty for a few seconds, then looked up at the ceiling,

"You don't hate me, do you?" he asked aloud to the man upstairs.

"No talking, you!" Molly said firmly, "Now, walk over here slowly. I want to watch my sexy man approach me… That's it, nice and slow, now before we get to it, and man, are we going to get to it, I, I want you to kiss it, I want you to kiss me down there and make me all warm and soft before you take control and ravage me as only you can."

"Your wish is…"

She cut him off, "No talking!" and with that Tommy did as he was told and nestled his head in between Molly's legs and kissed and licked her until she begged him to stop. He slowly moved his way up her body, running his tongue along her belly past her belly button to her neck, over her chin to her mouth, but then pulled back from kissing her and paused a moment for effect.

He stared deep into her eyes for several seconds as she stared back into his, and then, in one thrust, aggressively inserted himself into her. Both gasped aloud with the extreme pleasure they simultaneously felt, and Tommy began to pound himself into her at a moderate rhythmic pace.

Within a couple of minutes, Molly was climaxing for the second time, and as she did, she wrapped herself around him with her arms and legs tightly and began to beg him,

"Yes, yes, yes, Tommy, oh my god, yes, take me, take me." She said again and again before she said, "Finish now! Cum, cum with me, Tommy, cum with me!" At which time he simply couldn't last any longer, the excitement and passion were too much, and they both collapsed in bed, panting and gasping for air.

Chapter Five

Tommy's eyes opened to the sound of the song "Cutting Out" by The Split Seconds playing as his phone alarm. It was 5:00 a.m. He wanted to get up early so he could get to his mother's place for a decent change of clothes before he made his way to the precinct.

He turned his phone off and rolled over to see Molly's beautiful green eyes staring back at him with a soft smile.

"Kiss me before you go, lover. I'll be dreaming of last night all day today."

Tommy kissed her, then pulled the covers up tighter to her chin and kissed her again on the head. He went back to the kitchen, where his clothes lay in a pile, got dressed, then returned to the bedroom and kissed Molly one more time before leaving.

By 5:30, he was quietly letting himself into his mother's apartment on 88th, only to find his mother awake in front of the television with a coffee in her hand, a cigarette in her mouth, and his best friend, little JoJo, hopping up and down in the entryway of the apartment in eager anticipation of seeing Tommy again.

"Ma, come on, it's five-thirty in the morning, and you're smoking already?"

"What difference does it make, Tommy? Five-thirty in the morning or five thirty in the
evening, smoking is smoking, Tommy, and I like it; besides, nothing goes better with a cup of coffee than a
tasty cigarette, Tommy, you should know that by now."

Tommy held little JoJo up, "And how you doing? How's my buddy doing today?"

"He's doing good, Tommy. He's a good, good boy, and I'm happy you finally decided to get us a dog. He's such a pleasure to have around, Tommy."

Maria couldn't see Tommy cock his head or make the face he made at her from behind, thinking, 'I finally decided? My whole life, I have wanted a dog, lady, and you always said no dogs. Now this one falls into our lap because I'm a sucker for a suffering animal, and you want to know why it took me so long to get a dog?' But he stayed silent, petted and scratched JoJo for a second, then kissed his mother Maria on the head,

"I'm going to hop in the shower and get changed for work, Ma."

"Work? I thought you was on vacation this week, Tommy?"

"I am, well, I was, but something happened, and I had to come back to hopefully straighten it out."

"You talking about that Southerland boy murdering the Spanish boy in the park, Tommy?" Maria asked casually,

never taking her eyes off the television
before taking another drag from her cigarette.

Tommy stopped. He was a little surprised, even taken
aback by his mother's question, "What do you know about
that, Ma?"

"Not much, Tommy. A couple of the girls at mass
were talking about it, Tommy. Said it was a grizzly
killing." Maria took another drag from her cigarette. "Said it was
Queenie Southerland's boy that done it, Tommy. That they
picked him up at his apartment, Tommy; no one
was surprised."

"No one was surprised, Ma?" He asked as he sat on the
sofa next to her recliner.

"Nah, no one, Tommy, you know, he's a
Southerland, Tommy, and he hangs around with that snake, that
old friend of yours, Terry Calahan, and his crew of filth up on
92nd Street. I tell you; it was smart you went in the Army when
you were young, Tommy. Got you away from that element; it
made a man out of you, Tommy. It kept you honest and clean
and strong." Then she took a deep drag from her cigarette, her
eyes still never leaving the television.

"What more did they say? And who? Which of your
friends was talking about this murder?"

"Oh, it was Bridey, and Nora, Tommy, I saw them at
mass, Tommy, and they told me that Queenie
Southerland's boy did it."

"Did they have any reason why, Ma? Any details, or maybe tell you where they heard it from?"

"Hmm? Bridey said the whole neighborhood was talking about it, Tommy. Well, of course, it was all over the news, you know. She said it was the Southerland boy and that the detectives picked him up over at their apartment, Tommy. That's about it, we were all just happy you boys caught him before he killed someone else, that's all," Maria then took her eyes off the television screen and put her hand on top of Tommy's, "God bless the NYPD, we all said, and then both Bridey and Nora thanked me for you, Tommy, and we said our own prayer and lit a candle for all of you on the force, and for that Spanish boy and his family too," and then she immediately turned back to the television and said, "And that was it, Tommy, that was it."

Tommy sat for a second and decided not to ask anymore. He knew that neighborhood gossip could often yield fruitful results, but he also did not want to let his mother know he was involved in this case.

This one was a little close to home, and he wouldn't want her to say anything to any of her friends or acquaintances that might jeopardize the case or his attempt to help Shane.

He stood and again kissed his mother on the head, then made his way to the bathroom for a shower and a shave. He got dressed, walked JoJo, kissed his mother goodbye, and headed off to the precinct to meet up with Mark.

Chapter Six

10:28 AM Horizon Juvenile Center 560 Brook Avenue, Bronx, NY

Tommy, Mark, and Queenie arrived together at the Horizon Juvenile Center and parked directly out front.

Horizon, a large imposing building of red brick and grey stone with grey steel trim, looked from the outside to be exactly what it was, a bad place to be. A place of lost souls, broken dreams, and maybe worst of all, a forlorn place for those who never had the chance to dream to begin with.

It was a newer, modern structure built in the late 1990s to replace its predecessor, the notorious Spafford, which had housed the city's youth offenders for decades before. Built to be an improvement to the traditional juvenile facilities, it soon became noted for its overcrowding and its violent, riotous attacks on staff, who were overwhelmed by the numbers of its growing population.

The three somberly entered the building and signed in for their scheduled meeting. They then took a seat as they waited for Shane's lawyer, Michael Rosen, to arrive.

Once he did, the four were brought to a
small meeting/interview room painted an institutional shade of
light green. In its center, there was a table, and four blue plastic
chairs were around it. Two more were sitting against the wall,
one of which Tommy immediately moved to the table.

He then intentionally sat Queenie at the head,
himself next to the right of her, and next to Mark on the same
side. Shane's lawyer sat across from Mark, leaving Shane's seat
to the left of his mother and directly across from Tommy.

A Corrections Officer soon entered the room and
led Shane in. Mark set a small recorder on the table to record
the interview.

Shane was dressed in his own clothes: a simple
crewneck sweatshirt, blue jeans, and white Adidas Superstar
sneakers. He had a small bruise under his left eye and an
abrasion on the middle knuckle of his right
hand. Tommy, Queenie, and Mark all immediately noticed these
injuries, but they seemed to slip past his counsel,
Michael Rosen.

"Are we ready, counsel?" Mark asked.

"Yes, sure, you may proceed," Rosen responded.

"Alright then," Mark started, "I know you remember
me, Shane, and I believe you know my partner
here, Detective Keane?"

"Yeah… How you doing, Keane?" Shane replied with a
face of stone and the demeanor of a man more than twice his
age.

Queenie immediately corrected him, "Detective Keane to you."

"Detective Keane," he paused momentarily, "No disrespect intended, Detective."

"None taken, Shane. How you makin' out in here? Looks like you been scrappin' a little?"

"Doing alright, first night a couple of older kids thought they were going to punk me up over dinner, you know, flex on the new white boy, but I straightened their asses right out."

Tommy smiled approvingly and gave the slightest of nods. "Was that it?"

"Yeah, I think they thought I was gonna be a push over, but you know these hood rats, Detective Keane, they may be tough on the outside, but none of them ever train, so when they get tagged by someone who can actually use his hands, well, kinda knocks the thug right out of them, I know you know the type?"

Tommy again smiled approvingly. Mark cocked his head, somewhat amazed by how unbelievably mature and collected this young thirteen-year-old was. Rosen didn't seem to take notice. Queenie remained silent and expressionless. Her boy was talking like a man, to men, and she was proud to see his current situation had not shaken him in the least; in fact, his attitude put her more at ease with the predicament he was currently in.

Mark asked, "I know you didn't want to talk to me on the night of your arrest, Shane, but we've spoken at length with your mother, and we have your counsel present as well, so are you willing to talk to me today?"

"I been talking, ain't I?"

"Shane." Queenie said lowly but firmly.

"Yes, sir, Detective Stein, I am willing to talk to you today."

"Okay then, can you tell us where you were on the evening of the Antonio Canales killing?"

"I was home."

"Alone?"

"Yup… Yes, Detective, home alone."

"Any way you can prove that to us?"

"Not here and now, no, but I guarantee if you do some kind of investigating, you'll find I was playing a video game with a group. I don't know how you guys will figure that out, but I'm sure you have your ways."

"You seem confident in our abilities, Shane," Mark said as he began to admire this young man's composure.

"I am. I'm also positive you have some way of pinpointing my phone somehow. I know it's a burner, but I'm sure you guys have your ways."

Holding back a smile, Queenie raised one eyebrow and glanced at Mark, knowing her son was holding his own.

"Why," Mark paused, "Why do you carry a burner phone, Shane?"

"Because they are cheap, and my mother doesn't want me watching porn or playing games on the internet, so she won't buy me a real phone. She's afraid those things may corrupt me and stunt my social development… I'm her only son, and she's deeply protective of me, Detective."

Rosen smiled; he liked the way this interview was going so far.

"I can appreciate that, Shane," Mark continued. "Tell me, please, about Antonio Canales and how you know him."

"I know him from the neighborhood and school."

"And?"

"And not a lot more. He's like two years older than me; we got different friends. I never really hung out with him; I had a small beef with him, maybe around last October? But we straightened that out, and there was no hard feelings. You know he was just a guy from around; if I saw him, I'd say what's up, and he'd do the same."

"Beef? Please give me the story there."

"Nothin' to it really, a couple of us were hanging out by the entrance to the Wagner schoolyard, sitting on the steps, and he told me to get the F out of his way, so I told him to watch his mouth, and he started talking tough… You know he was with another friend and two girls and wanted to show off."

"And then what?"

"I stood up and probably cursed at him, and he grabbed me by my shirt and got right up in my face, so I headbutted him and then punched him like two or three times, knocking him down the steps to the pavement… But then it was over, and like maybe a few days later, we shook hands, and he even said sorry and that he asked for it."

"So, no lingering animosity?"

"Lingering animosity? You mean was we still mad at each other?"

"Yes, that's exactly what I mean, Shane."

"No, sir, no, Detective, none of that, we got along just fine after that, in fact, I couldn't tell you when but the last time I seen Tony was maybe two weeks ago, and he bummed a cigarette off me and we talked for a minute, and no, no animosity was present from neither of us."

Mark paused for a moment, "What size shoes do you wear, Shane?"

"Eight."

"What brand sneakers do you wear, Shane?"

"Adidas."

"Do you wear any other sneakers or footwear?"

"Nah, not really, I got some Timbos, if it snows, but really only Adidas, and, and only the shell tops." The last part he emphasized.

"Superstars," Tommy interjected flatly.

"Yeah, them, Superstar shell tops."

"Who… Can you tell me about Tony's friends? Who he hangs with at school or from the neighborhood?"

"He's got a close friend, Georgio, that everyone calls G, another kid named Mike, I don't know their last names, he's always got some girls hanging around him too, one named Siri, the others I don't know."

"Popular kid?"

"Yeah, I would say yeah, definitely."

"Anyone you know would like to hurt Tony? Any rumors about him
running around the neighborhood or school?"

"No, like I said he was pretty popular, in fact, the only person I know who ever had beef with Tony was me, and I told you about that, that was the only time, he got fresh with me and we got into it in the school yard, and that was it, over, done, none of that fuckin animosity shit."

"Language." Said Queenie.

"Sorry, no animosity at all, we got along fine after that."

"So, you're telling me you didn't kill Tony Canales two nights ago."

Both Shane and Queenie furrowed their brows, showing a bit of anger at the question, Queenie opening her mouth but before any words came out Shane answered him, "That's right, and when you check that phone you took from me and do whatever it is you do with it and with my Xbox, I'm sure you will see, I was nowhere near that park, and I was at home like I said I was."

"You seem quite confident, Shane."

"I am more than confident, Detective Stein. You got the wrong guy, and you're going to find that out, and you know what, Detective?

"What's that?"

"I won't have no animosity when you do. I know you got a job to do, and I know someone pointed a finger at me, and you maybe had no choice but to pick me up. I don't like it, but I get it."

The five of them then wrapped up the interview. Shane was taken back to his cell after a long embrace with his mother, who promised him he would be home soon, and Tommy and Mark returned an almost silent Queenie Southerland back to her apartment.

On the way to the precinct from Queenie's block, Tommy remained silent until Mark said.

"I think you're right, Tom; I think we might have grabbed the wrong kid here."

"I couldn't see him doing it, and I feel even stronger now. In fact, if I thought he was guilty before, I think he may have changed my mind today."

"No doubt, in fact, in all my years of policing, I don't think I've ever met a cooler, more confident character than young Shane here. If he's not innocent, that performance was worthy of an Academy Award."

Chapter Seven

Tommy and Mark returned to the precinct, sat in the squad room, and went over everything they had in Antonio Canales' case folder. Both read over the statements given by the young ladies, Iyana Franco and Stephanie McCrain, and as Mark had said, both statements were pretty scant. Iyana's statement read;

"I saw a boy I know named Shane run from Carl Schurz Park and across East End Avenue, along with three other boys that I did not know. I also know that Shane hated Tony and that they had had fights in the past."

Stephanie McCrain's statement read;

"Me and Iyana, was walking up East End Avenue and saw a boy we knew named Shane and three boys that we didn't know, and they all come out of the park together, and that's all."

Tommy looked up at Mark, "I thought these statements were scant; they're almost nonexistent."

"I know, but both girls were certain it was Shane, who they both knew from school and the neighborhood, and that, along with Shane's name written on the pavement, prompted us to move on him. We got his name and address from his school. When we grabbed him he was of course wearing size eight sneakers, couple that with this kids hard as nails attitude, and refusing to say a word, his mother's history, and both of their connections to the Calahan Crew, not to mention the fact that neither of them, nor their lawyer, could muster any defense for him other than "You got the wrong kid!" - Well, there wasn't not only little doubt we had the right kid, but no other visible avenue to take at the time."

"I get it, but now… and correct me if I'm wrong, we have some doubts, and we need to dig deeper into this case because there's a legitimate chance, we do indeed have the wrong kid."

"Yes, I don't think we can cut him loose yet, and I don't think ADA Schwartz would go for it, anyway, not until we can show her why we have our doubts and put a new direction on this investigation."

"I agree, let's get to it, I think we should get with as many friends and acquaintances as we can of both our victim and Shane, see if we can get some pings off of Shane's cell phone, and," Tommy paused and smiled for a moment, "Listen to me, I'm taking advice from a thirteen year old sitting in a cell in Horizon, but yeah, if Shane's right, and we can find out about his video game usage on the date and time of the homicide, if there is any such time stamp on his gaming that says he was indeed home, well then it looks like our boy does have an alibi?"

"Agreed… Alright, well, we have two names: Georgio and Siri. Both of these two were friends of Antonio, and both witnessed the fight in the schoolyard. It's getting late, but let's head over to their school. We can still make it in time to speak with someone in the office and get their phone numbers and addresses of record."

"Let's go."

3:54 PM Robert F. Wagner Junior High School 167, 220 East 76th Street.

Tommy and Mark entered the grand red doors of the building, the same Junior High that Tommy himself attended some thirty-three years prior. They identified themselves at the security desk to the right of the entrance that sat in front of the auditorium. Then, they turned around and made their way up the few steps into the corridor on the first floor of classrooms, where, to the left, were the administration offices.

Tommy felt odd walking these halls, he knew this school so well from the years he, Terry, and Queenie had all attended, he had so many memories, both good and not so good from those days, but during this visit everything seemed so much smaller and antiquated, and somehow he felt like a sinister trespasser, an adult stepping into the world of children that was no longer his own, a world he had a hard time identifying with.

They again identified themselves to a tiny grey-haired woman who called to a Miss Stefcheck to come and take care of them.

"Hello, hello, you? You are police detectives. Oh my, you must be here about Tony, I imagine." Michelle Stefcheck nervously asked.

"Yes, ma'am, we are. We're investigating Antonio's homicide and would like to know if you can help us out with the addresses and phone numbers for two of his friends, a Georgio and a Siri."

"Yes, yes, of course, I know both of those kids. Especially pleasant children, just like, oh my," she paused momentarily and wiped her eyes as she choked up a bit before continuing, "Just like Tony, oh my, he was such a lovely boy." She said before taking a large swallow to keep her emotions in check.

"So, you knew Tony?" Tommy asked.

"Yes, of course, he was such a nice boy."

"We'd like to ask you about him then, if we may?" Tommy asked again.

"Yes, please, Detectives, come in here and have a seat. I'll do my best to help you in any way I can."

Michelle Stefcheck led them behind the counter and into an office. She sat at her desk, and Mark and Tommy sat down in front of her.

"We are trying to find out more about Antonio, Miss Stefcheck. We know two of his friends were Giorgio and Siri, but beyond those two names, we have no one else to reach out to. Can you name any other friends or acquaintances of Antonio?"

"Tony was a rather popular young man, so he had lots of friends in school, but Georgio would definitely be the kid to talk to; they were both very close. He, Georgio, hasn't come back to school yet; he's a bit broken up over the loss.

"Is Siri Antonio's girlfriend?" Mark asked.

"I don't think so, she was always with Tony and Giorgio, but that Tony, well," Michelle paused and wiped a tear from her eye, "Tony was quite the charmer, he was always running around with different girls, he was handsome, and sweet and polite, so so well liked… I, I understand you … can I ask?"

"Please go ahead," Mark said.

"The rumor is, you made an arrest, and it's one of our students?"

"Yes, yes, we did. May I ask who you believe we arrested, Miss Stefcheck?"

Michelle Stefcheck leaned into her desk as far as she could and said in a loud whisper,

"I believe it's Shane Southerland."

"Yes, ma'am, we do have Shane Southerland in custody. What can you tell us about him?"

"Oh, Shane… Shane is a strange case, he, well he is constantly truant for one, but not disliked by other students or by staff, in fact, all his teachers seem to like him, he's a bit aloof, polite, but also surprisingly mature and very, I don't know, honest and blunt, when speaking to him it's more like speaking to a grown man, he's definitely got an edge to him, and after meeting his mother I think I know where he gets it, she seems like a tough cookie herself, but that being said, I would have never imagined he would be capable of something like this?"

"What can you tell us about his mother?" Tommy asked.

"Also, polite. I have only met her once. She is an attractive, well-dressed woman. I would guess she is incredibly successful at whatever she does. It seems like she is possibly or probably in charge of something. I don't know she has that A type personality, something about her though, besides that her son doesn't often make it to school, or that she doesn't seem concerned about his schooling at all, but there's something, as cordial as she is, that rubs me the wrong way, I don't know, Detective, she made me uncomfortable when we met."

"I can see that," Mark stated.

The three spoke for a bit more, but other than a brief overview of each boy and the contact information for Giorgio and Siri, Miss Stefcheck had nothing more to add to their investigation, so they headed back to the precinct.

***

As Tommy and Mark walked through the door of the Squad room, Doreen directed her hello towards Tommy, "Welcome back, Mr. Man, how was your vacation?"

"Good, Doreen, got some much-needed rest and relaxation in, ate well, hit the gym almost daily and got to spend a couple of days with my little girl… I didn't need more to tell you the truth."

"Excellent, and how is your Caitlyn?"

"She, well, she's the most beautiful thing ever, so sweet and so smart, and she seems to be rockin' it up there in Siena, so yeah, it was indeed wonderful to see her and catch up a little."

As Tommy and Doreen made small talk, Mark immediately got on the phone and began making arrangements to interview Giorgio and Siri. He also got in touch with Iyana and Michelle's parents and arranged for them to come in the next day as well.

Mark then went to the property clerk, signed out Shane's cell phone that he had vouchered for evidence, and brought it back up to the squad room.

"Hey, Tommy - Doreen, have either of you ever tried to track one of these burner phones? Is there any difference? "I know it can be done; I've just never done it," Mark asked as he took a seat at his desk.

"I never have," Doreen said. But I know it's essentially the same as any other phone. However, the phone company won't be able to tell you who it belongs to;

that, of course, is anonymous, which is the whole appeal of the burner."

"Yeah, well, in this case, we know who the phone belongs to; I want to confirm if this kid's got an alibi."

"Who's this, your teen killer from this weekend?"

"That's the one."

Tommy interjected, "Yes, I've done this several times. You'll need to send a subpoena to the company; they'll be able to track the number. I think it's called the IMEI number, which I think is the International Mobile Equipment ID number, like any other phone, and check for pings. That's what you're looking to do, right? You want to see if you can ping Shane to his block on the night of the murder rather than in the park, yeah?"

"Yes sir, we would have gotten to this eventually if it had ever gone to trial, and we needed to prove he was in the park, but now that we have some doubts about his guilt, I want to get the ball rolling on this, see what the pings will show us, and see if we do indeed have the wrong kid."

"You think Shane Southerland isn't your man, Mark?" Doreen asked.

"We have our doubts. The kid has a pretty confident and plausible argument, and I want to check it out."

"So, you were able to get him to talk?" Doreen asked, "I know when we snatched him up on Saturday, he was D&D." (Def & Dumb)

"Yeah, I brought Tommy up to Horizon, and the kid opened up. Tommy knew him from the Marshall case back in November, and he trusted him. I wish he had trusted me. If he's innocent, he'd possibly be free by now."

Mark paused for a moment in thought, then asked both Tommy and Doreen, "Either of you know anything about video games?

"No, has never been my thing," Tommy replied. You're asking if we can track his usage, yes? Like he mentioned, we could."

"Yes, exactly."

"I game a little. What's the question?" asked Doreen.

"Shane claims he was home alone playing video games. Do you know if we subpoena the gaming company, if there is any way they could tell us if he was indeed playing games at a certain hour on a certain day?"

Doreen looked back at both Mark and Tommy for a second. She smiled and then began, "You two truly are a couple of dinosaurs, aren't you? If this kid was playing a game at the time of the murder, and well, it would depend on the game, and if, as most gamers do, he saved it, there would be a time stamp right on the game itself. No subpoena necessary, no searching necessary; it will be right there on the game files."

Tommy and Mark looked at each other, almost in disbelief. They were, indeed, dinosaurs. Not only did they not know this simple fact, but they also struggled to comprehend what Doreen was explaining. All they knew was that she knew.

"What are you doing right now?" Mark asked Doreen.

"I'm typing up some follow-ups on these cases."

"Come on, we're taking a ride."

The three of them put on their jackets and began to make their way down the precinct's stairs. As they did, Mark called Queenie Southerland.

"Hello, Miss Southerland, Detective Stein, 21st Precinct here. Are you home? … How quickly can you be there? We may have doubts about your son Shane being mixed up in this homicide, but we need to get back into his room and check on something. Can you meet us there? -Fifteen minutes? -Perfect, we'll be there.

6:33 PM Shane's bedroom

Doreen sat in Shane's chair and pulled herself up to the desk where his gaming console and monitor were placed. Tommy, Mark, and Queenie stood behind her, watching intently. She turned the system on and was pleased to see that it was a game she had played herself.

"Ooh, Skyrim." She said out loud.

"What's that mean?" Mark asked.

"It's an open-world fantasy RPG, which means Shane is cool!" She then turned to face the three standing behind her and said in a lower, more solemn voice, "Skyrim belongs to the Nords." Then she returned to the game, leaving the trio perplexed by her statement.

She loaded Shane's saved game files and then told Mark to come closer. "Here, Mark, you see here," she said, pointing with her finger. It was the time stamp she had described. "Right here, he didn't lie. Someone was playing this game at the time we believe the attacks occurred.

"He's innocent; I knew it, and he told you, he told you he was here playing that stupid fucking game," Queenie said in an anxious tone, letting her guard down for a moment, sounding almost more relieved than confident. "What's next? When does my Shane come home?" she then asked.

"We're going to have to take this game for evidence, then see what we get back from the phone company, and then present this information to the District Attorney's office, hopefully, if everything goes smoothly, we'll be able to have Shane back home in a day or two, but please understand, we have to get permission from the District Attorney's office, that being said I think, and I think Detective Stein will agree, it's looking pretty promising that Shane will be released within the next twenty-four to forty-eight hours?"

Mark continued, "Yes, yes, Miss Southerland, we will need to corroborate what we've seen here today with what the phone company says, then present it to the ADA in charge of this case, but I am feeling positive. We should be able to have Shane home tomorrow, if not by the next day; it just may take a bit of time.

"I don't know what to feel. Am I supposed to be grateful for your help, or angry as hell with you for arresting him in the first place?" Was Queenie's response.

Chapter Eight

After signing out for the day, Tommy began walking uptown. His original intent was to call Molly and, if she was free, take her out for some drinks and maybe a repeat of the night they had just spent together. If she were working, he would stop by the bar for a couple of beers and then maybe a bite to eat and, again, enjoy a repeat of the night they had just spent together, a night that had certainly made an imprint.

This thought weighed on Tommy somewhat. He had become exceedingly fond of Molly over the last few months; how could he not? She was physically beautiful, bright, funny, and sassy. He honestly loved everything about her, and he knew she was crazy about him; she had, after all, while berating him on the street a few weeks before, actually let the L word slip through her lips during her rant.

Tommy knew it was Molly who approached him sexually; he knew he allowed her to chart the course of this relationship of theirs, and thus far, he was enjoying the ride. But now, now that he had genuine feelings for this woman and truly wanted the best for her, he knew he would have to end the relationship sooner rather than later.

It had been gnawing at him for some time. The age difference was too significant, and she deserved better. He was too old and his life too complicated to start another family, and to him, it was an unquestionable black-and-white issue. If he couldn't give her everything, he should step aside, give her nothing, and let her get on with her life.

He knew she was too young and full of so much life and potential that it was simply wrong to waste more time with a man who was almost twice her age. He could never give her the time, the stability, and frankly, the future that she not only deserved but that he desperately wanted her to have, even if she, as of yet, didn't want these things for herself.

So, with these thoughts whirling around in his head as he walked up Lexington Avenue, he decided that instead of making that call, he would grab a quick bite at the Don Filippo Pizzeria on Lexington and 78th, then head over to his mother's and watch some television with her and little JoJo. It may not have been as exciting an option, but he felt it was the right thing to do.

Tommy grabbed a spot in the back of the pizzeria and ordered a Chicken Parm Hero on garlic bread and an unsweetened iced tea. As he sat and ate, he watched a young couple in their mid-twenties, a few tables over, enjoying their meals and each other's company; love was in their eyes. He had no idea who they were or if they would last, but he did know they had a chance. He also knew that Molly had no future with him, not in the big picture, not in the long run. He knew she was wasting her time with him.

Tommy finished his sandwich, ordered two tiramisus to go, and then headed home to his mother's place.

When he arrived, he took an anxious and excited JoJo for a walk around the block, and the three of them settled in for some television. Tommy, of course, let his mother, Maria, choose the film, which turned out to be Mermaids, starring Cher, Winona Ryder, and Bob Hoskins.

They sat and watched, enjoying their tiramisu. Little JoJo cuddled with Tommy for the first half of the film, then got up and jumped onto Maria's lap. She tucked him into his usual spot, between her thigh and the arm of her recliner, and covered him with the quilt that lay across her lap.

By the time the movie ended, it was almost 11:00 p.m., and Maria was obviously tired. Tommy helped her up and walked her to her room, kissing her head and saying goodnight. He then took JoJo out for another walk around the block before returning home and going to bed himself.

- 88 -

Chapter Nine

Tommy's eyes opened to the pitch-blackness of his room. He checked his phone; it would be forty-plus minutes before his alarm would sound, but he felt great, so he rolled out of bed in the dark and banged out his fifty morning pushups.

He then got up on his knees and switched his bedside lamp on to see little JoJo sitting up, staring at him with an eager look on his face, so he pulled on some sweatpants and a hoodie, slipped on some sneakers, and stuffed his .38 Centennial five shot pistol into his pocket and stepped out of his room to take JoJo for his first walk of the day.

His mother was already up, sitting in her recliner with the news on, a coffee in hand, and the smell of a recently smoked cigarette in the air.

"Morning, Ma, how you doing today?"

"Doing good, Tommy. Can I fix you some breakfast, Tommy?"

"You sure can, Ma. How about a little oatmeal? You know how I like it. I'll be right back. Let me take this boy around the block."

"Go ahead, you two. Take your time, Tommy. I'll have your breakfast ready for you when you get back."

After his walk and oatmeal, Tommy sat with his mother for about half an hour before showering, shaving, dressing for the day, and heading out the door. He stopped on the stoop and scanned the block from left to right, then stepped off and headed toward Second Avenue.

It was a dark, cloudy morning, and it looked like rain. As he made it to the avenue, a cold sprinkle began, so he hailed a cab and arrived at the precinct just as a heavy rain started to fall.

Although he arrived at work about twenty-five minutes early, he found Mark already there, scribbling on a yellow pad.

"What's the plan for today, Mark?" Tommy asked.

"Well, we have those four kids coming in today. I have them spaced out in two-hour intervals: nine, eleven, one, then three, so that should eat up the entire day. I sent the subpoena to the phone company and am hoping to hear back from them today as well."

"Well, alright then. I'm yours today, my friend. If there's anything you need done, please let me know. If not, I'll be right here, going through and catching up on some of my older cases until these interviews arrive."

∗∗∗

8:58 AM The Siri Webster Interview

Mark sat Siri Webster, a small, pretty, blonde girl of fifteen, down in the far chair of the interview room. She wore a red hoodie under a pink denim jacket, blue jeans, and UGG boots. Her mother was next to her, an attractive woman in her early forties, also wearing jeans and a hoodie. Both had pleasant yet quiet demeanors and were eager to help.

Mark sat in a chair opposite the ladies, and Tommy on the bench that ran along the wall beside the table.

"Thank you so much for making it in this morning, ladies; we appreciate it," Mark began, "You, of course, know what we're here to talk about. I want to gather as much information as I can about both Antonio and Shane and maybe get to know both of them a little better through you, Siri. Do you think you can help Detective Keane and me with that?"

"Yes," Siri said rather demurely, "What would you like to know?"

"First, tell me about Antonio. It sounds like you two were close friends."

"Yeah, we were very good friends. We met sitting together at the same desk in 7th-grade homeroom, and we just, you know, hit it off, you know,
we liked the same music, liked the same games and TV shows, and he was so nice, Tony was a truly nice boy."

"How close were you? Did you ever date, may I ask?"

"No, we never dated, or kissed or made out, or anything like that; we kind of, well, somehow, we were kind of actually too close for that if that makes sense; we were more like best friends."

"And your friend Giorgio, how did he fit in?"

"Giorgio was the same. We were like, I don't know, three pieces of the same pie, we all started here together and it just, you know, the three of us clicked, we all got along from the beginning, Tony was so like, charismatic, and so popular, and G, was the funny one, just, he is so funny and fun to be around, and well, I guess I would be the smart one, you know the bookworm and music nerd, and we jelled, we do everything together, even if one of us has some kind of girlfriend or in my case boyfriend like I do right now, it's always still been us three, you know, always…"

"So, you have a boyfriend now, does Giorgio, and did Tony, I haven't heard of him having a girlfriend yet."

"G was dating a girl for about six months, but she moved to Brooklyn, and well, that just didn't work, and Tony…" Siri paused for a moment, "Sorry Mom… there's no other way to say it; Tony was a slut, I mean, I'm sure you can understand, he was so beautiful, it's like every girl wanted him, and it's not that he took advantage of them, so much as well, he took advantage of the situation, everybody loved Tony, even the teachers would flirt with him, it was almost sickening the attention he would get from women."

"And that didn't go to his head? Was he ever, I don't know, was he conceited?" Mark asked.

"No, not really. I think that was part of why we
all loved him so much; he was absolutely beautiful, yeah, but he
was also such a nice, I mean truly a nice person to be around."

"But no steady girlfriend, at the moment anyway."

"No, he was never serious about girls, he was, like I
said, a slut," she turned to her mother and asked, "Tell them
what grandpa said about Tony, Mom."

Siri's mother put on a faint smile and, mimicking her
father, said, "That boy's got a girl for every finger on both his
hands."

"Because every time my grandpa saw him in the street,
he'd be with some other girl."

"Was he ever in trouble at home or school, any drugs or
alcohol?"

"No, never. Tony was a good, good person, and to be
honest, I think he liked himself too much to drink or do drugs.
I mean, yes, an occasional beer and an occasional smoke, but
rarely, I mean almost never."

"Okay, tell me what you know about Shane?"

"Shane is the piece of shit that killed my best
friend," Siri replied with controlled contempt.

"Have you always disliked Shane, Siri?"

"Actually, no, I haven't. We have never been close, but
we know each other from the neighborhood, and from school,
he's a year behind us in school, so we've never been in
class together, but we do have some mutual friends, you know

how that goes, so like our paths do and have crossed many
times."

"So, please tell me about him."

"Shane is kinda quiet, keeps to himself, mostly just
hangs out with his friends Joey, and an Irish kid named
Decland, and we know them all from around.
Sometimes we'll all end up at some party together, I don't know
what to tell you really, like I know him but just from around,
you know, he's behind us a grade in school, and I'll see
him around the neighborhood and parties, or the movies
or whatever and we'll like, say hello, but that's about it."

"I understand there was a problem
between Shane and Tony that resulted in a fight a little while
ago?"

"Yes, I was there for that."

"Can you tell us about it?"

"Stupid boy stuff, Shane and Joey and that kid Declan
were all sitting on the steps of the schoolyard,
and Tony for whatever stupid reason decided to tell them to get
out of his way, which like, wasn't really necessary, there was
room enough to get around them but he was, Tony was like
trying to be cool in front of these two girls, and well, okay, I'll
tell you one thing, Shane is not a kid you can push around okay,
he won't take shit from anyone, and he will stand up to anyone,
even if he knows he's going to lose, and he stood up
to Tony and Tony grabbed him and Shane just punched him
out, I know he's only like thirteen, but he'll tell you he does
boxing and I believe it."

"So, they hated each other after that?"

"I would say yes because of what recently happened, but like, no, because I know they made friends afterward and shook hands and everything seemed cool until, well, until last week."

The interview went on a bit longer, but there wasn't much more Siri could add to the investigation, so Mark and Tommy again thanked the ladies for coming in and then waited for the following interview to begin.

"Lovely girl," Tommy commented to Mark as Siri and her mother left the room.

"Yes, they seemed very nice, and I love seeing a mother and daughter getting along so well together. Great interview. My wife has always been that way with my kids, and I'm so happy about it. I just wish Siri had a little more to offer, though, something we could run with, you know?"

"Well, we got three more to go, Mark, hopefully someone will drop a lead or two?"

11:08 AM The Georgio Montenegro Interview

Mark and Tommy took the same seats as before, with Georgio, a tall, thin, relatively handsome young man with a thick head of black hair and a pencil-thin mustache, dressed from head to toe in black. His father, Lazlo, a shorter, rounder, balding man of fifty-five, took the same seats as Siri and her mother.

The interview began with the same basic questions. Giorgio, however, was not nearly as composed as Siri had been and, from the beginning, began to break down, sometimes crying uncontrollably when asked questions about his dead best friend, Antonio.

But through almost an hour of sobs, tears, and occasional outbursts and rants, several statements were taken note of:

"I can't believe this! I can't believe he killed him. They were supposed to be friends; they got along so well, how, how in the world could he do that to his friend?"

"Nah, no way they were fighting over girls, Tony didn't give a shit about any one girl, for him it was more about, shit, more about just having fun with all the girls, you know, he didn't have time to commit to one, and didn't care about any, and Shane was more into his gangsta shit, and his wannabe boxing shit, nah I don't think he killed him for no girl, I can't see that."

"Nah, until this happened, I thought they was friends. Yeah, they had a fight once, but that was nothin'."

"Nah, definitely no drugs. Tony was too conceited for drugs, you feel me? And Shane was too much of an athlete."

"Yeah, we all know Shane killed him, everybody knows that, but I can't figure out why. And that's what's killing me, man. Why, why would Shane do this? It don't make no sense to me!"

The detectives thanked the men for coming in for the interview, then sat down and discussed the two they had

just spoken with at length as they awaited the
third interviewee to show up.

Mark began, "Listening to these kids and reading over
my notes, neither of them incriminated Shane in the least. In
fact, I think although they both believe he is
guilty, neither seems to believe it could be him."

"Exactly, they're buying the story they've heard, but I
bet you anything if they weren't told that story, and we asked
them who had done it, they would have never picked Shane."

1:12 PM The Iyana Franco Interview

Mark and Tommy sat one of their scheduled
interviewees down in the room for the third time that day. This
time, it was Iyana Franco, who was a short, round young
woman of fifteen, with her black hair pulled straight back in a
tight ponytail. She wore a black zip-up hoodie over a maroon t-
shirt with matching maroon pants and black sneakers.

Her mother, Lucia, was also an extremely short,
stocky, round woman who wore a long tan cardigan over
a black t-shirt and jeans. Neither appeared very happy to return
for this interview.

"Hello, ladies. Thank you so much for coming back. I
know we just sat here a few days ago, but time was limited. As I
mentioned, we would probably have some follow-up questions
for you, and here we are today."

"It's fine, Detective Stein; we know this is
important." Mrs. Franco replied.

"Alright, so we know you saw Shane leaving the park last week with three other boys. That was your statement the other night, right, Iyana?"

"Yeah, that's right," she replied.

"You recognized Shane, but can you name any of the other boys?"

"No, like I said the other day, I only knew Shane."

"Okay, I was hoping, after thinking about it for a few days, maybe you'd know more?"

"No, only Shane."

"And how do you know Shane?"

"I know him from around the neighborhood and from school. Most everyone knows Shane."

"Do you two run around in the same circle?"

"No, definitely not," Iyana replied with a bit of contempt.

"I take it you don't like Shane?"

"No, not particularly. I don't think there's much to like; he, well, he's a criminal for one."

"Really? Please tell me more. What crimes has he committed?"

"Besides murdering Tony in cold blood, he," she paused and looked at her mother, "Can I say it, Mom?" Her mother nodded, "He's a Calahan."

Mark, knowing precisely what she was saying but wanting more from her, played coy and furrowed his brow. Then he pushed his glasses up onto his face and said, "No, his name is Southerland Iyana, not Calahan."

"I know his name is Southerland, but he's a Calahan; he's part of the Calahan gang from 92nd Street over by the projects; you're the police. You have to know what I'm saying?"

"Oh, the Calahan gang, yes, I've heard of them. You mean to tell me this thirteen-year-old boy is a member of the Calahan gang?"

"Yes, that's exactly what I'm telling you, like, he's deep in with them."

"And what kind of things does he do for them?"

Iyana looked at her mother, who again nodded. "He sells or delivers drugs and guns and steals things. You know, doing robberies and things like that."

"Okay, then, this is news to us. Now, what can you tell me about Shane and Tony? Do you have any idea what happened to make Shane kill Tony?"

"They never liked each other; I can only think it was jealousy. I think Shane hated Tony because he was so handsome, and all the girls liked him. I know they had a fight a while ago, and Shane always said he won, but I bet he didn't actually win it. I bet he's lying; Tony was older, bigger, and stronger than Shane, so I think, yeah, I think it was all just jealousy."

"Were you friends with Tony?"

"Yes, we were friends, for sure. I don't think I would say close friends, but he was kind of in our friend group, and I've known him for most of my life."

"But obviously not friends with Shane?"

"God no, but you know, I would still see him at parties and around the neighborhood. I mean, we weren't enemies until now."

"Until now?"

"Yeah, now that he killed Tony, I absolutely hate him!"

"I know I've already asked this, but I want to ask you again, and please try to remember: Can you tell me what Shane was wearing the night you saw him?"

"No, I don't remember. I saw those boys running from the park like I told you last week, and I knew or recognized that one face, and that was Shane."

"And nothing's changed then. You haven't been able to put a name to any of the other boys?"

"No, I wish I could, Detective Stein, but I can't. I don't know any of the others."

"Thank you, ladies; I may still be in touch, and please, please, if you remember anything else, contact me immediately.

"Yes, sir, we will." Mrs. Franco answered, "And thank you both for your service to our neighborhood, we do appreciate you."

2:55 PM The Stephanie McCrain Interview

Stephanie McCrain, also fifteen, was a relatively tall young lady at five feet nine; she had long reddish-blond hair that was parted in the middle and hung straight down. She had a noticeable overbite and a dull look in her eyes; she was dressed in a simple grey V-neck sweater, tight blue jeans, and white sneakers.

Her mother, Mary Kate, forty, was also tall and thin. Her hair, too, was a reddish blonde, which she wore pulled back on the sides but loose in the back. Tommy recognized her from the neighborhood, but it seemed apparent that she didn't recognize him.

Again, they all sat the same way as everyone else had in the interview room, and Mark began.

"Let me thank you, ladies, for coming in today. I know we just spoke a couple of days ago, but as I said, I would have more questions, so here we are again. Now, Stephanie, please, if you will, tell me again what you saw last week when you were with Iyana."

"We saw Shane run out of the park with three other guys."

"And did you recognize any of the other guys?"

"Nope, didn't know none of them except for Shane."

"Okay, and how do you know Shane?"

"You know, from like around and like from school."

"And how about Tony? How did you know him?"

"Same, like from around and like school."

"Do you like Shane?"

"No, I don't."

"Why not?"

"Cause he's mean, likes to pick on people and say names."

It was becoming evident that Stephanie was not a bright girl. The dull gaze in her eyes never seemed to change, and she spoke rather slowly and in a childlike manner not befitting her age.

"Does he call you names?"

"Yeah."

"Do you want to tell me what he calls you, Stephanie?"

Stephanie pursed her lips; she was obviously not happy to repeat it, but she did as she was asked.

"He calls me Shadoof; he named me that a long time ago now, and so because of that, everyone knows me as Shadoof, or Doofy Stephanie, sometimes Stephdoof, but mostly Shadoof, and I hate it."

"I'm sorry, dear. That wasn't very nice at all. Now, how about Tony? Did you like Tony?

Stephanie pursed her lips again, this time tighter and for longer. Her eyes squinted, and tears started to roll down her cheeks.

"Yes, I liked Tony." She took a deep breath. He was always friendly to me. He never called me Shadoof after I told him I didn't like it. And I think what happened to him is the worst. I wish it didn't happen. I think I'm going to be sad and miss him forever. It's the worst thing in my life right now."

With that, her emotions let loose, and she began to cry uncontrollably. It was obvious that she was in a state that was not going to be conducive to continuing the interview, so Mark apologized to Stephanie and her mother, Mary Kate, and gave his condolences as best he could to Stephanie. He also asked again if they would please reach out to him if any new information became available on their end.

Mary Kate McCrain said she absolutely would be back, then apologized for the situation, and Stephanie continued to cry as they left the Squad Room.

Chapter Ten

The end of the tour had come, and no word had come in as far as the cell phone company was concerned, so Shane would spend another night in Horizon.

Both Tommy and Mark signed out for the day, and as Tommy began walking uptown, he pulled out his phone and called Queenie.

"Tommy Keane?" Is how she answered.

"Hey, Queens, how you makin out?"

"I been better, but you know, I also been a whole lot worse."

"Can we meet real quick?"

"Sure, I'm over at Phil Hughes. I'll be here for the next couple of hours. Do you want to come by?"

Tommy paused. "Yeah Queens, I'm on my way." Phil Hughes Pub was a longtime Yorkville establishment, almost kitty-corner from his mother's building on 88th Street and visible from her stoop.

A place Tommy had often frequented years before, but probably hadn't been inside for almost twenty years or more.

His avoidance had nothing to do with the bar or staff itself; it was because it had remained a stronghold of a deeply cliquey bunch of neighborhood types, like his two dear friends, Terry and Queenie, and all of their hangabouts. It was a life he had left at seventeen when he joined the Army, and a world he had tried to divorce himself from completely since joining the police department.

Phil Hughes Pub opened in 1957; it was an ample room with a long bar, a pool table, a dart board, and beautiful terrazzo floors that Tommy always admired. They kept the place very clean, and although the neighborhood had changed so much around it, Phil Hughes Pub was able to remain a neighborhood gin mill, very much like Tommy's favorite haunt, Bailey's Corner had.

It was a little too close to home for him, and that had nothing to do with its proximity to his mother's apartment but with a large portion of its clientele.

***

Tommy made his way up 1st Avenue to the Phil Hughes Pub, which was on the southwest corner of 1st and 88th. As he stepped inside, it was exactly as he remembered it from some 20 years prior.

There was a handful of customers in the front of the bar, typical working stiffs in for an after-work beer or cocktail before finding their way home.

To the left sat Queenie Southerland, the queen of the neighborhood, holding court. She sat on a bar stool at a high-top table, a thin older man of about sixty stood in front of her, nodding, yes. Her face was expressionless. Then, she handed the older man several folded bills. Tommy assumed it was a loan of some sort, and the man's tentative nodding was him agreeing to terms.

Further to his left in the corner sat Michael and Jamie Devine, known around Yorkville as 'The Brothers Devine.' Two toughs who handled most of Queenie's and Terry's dirty work, they stared intently at Tommy with contempt. It wasn't that they necessarily had contempt for him or for the police; mostly, they had contempt for the world as a whole.

They knew and respected Tommy as a stand-up guy from the neighborhood, but as a cop, they also saw him as an enemy, someone who played for the wrong side, and, in general, as a threat.

Nonetheless, both gave a slight nod when Tommy made eye contact, silently acknowledging his presence and his membership to the sacredness of what was considered 'The old neighborhood.'

As the older gentleman stepped away from Queenie, another working stiff in his mid-to-late fifties approached her but stopped dead in his tracks as she lifted one index finger, giving him the sign to wait. She then nodded to Tommy and gave him a little wave to come join her.

As he approached, she stood up and took a step forward to give him a long, hard embrace, followed by a kiss on the mouth, "Oh, Tommy, how I have missed you; I so wish you weren't a stranger to us anymore."

"I miss you too, Queens, I do, but you gotta understand, I…"

She put her index finger up to shush him, "Honey, I get it, I do, and I know you are doing what's right, avoiding everything we grew up to be; I get it, but it doesn't mean we can't still love you and miss you."

They stared deep into one another's eyes for a moment, and then she began again, "Quick, I know you don't want to be seen with me, so quick, what do you have to tell me, Tommy?"

"I wanted to keep you updated, and of course can't do it over the phone, but it's obvious we couldn't
spring Shane today, all we're waiting for is the phone company to answer the subpoena, and hopefully it will give us what we want, or the evidence we need to bring Shane home,
I wanted to tell you where we were, also we conducted some interviews with some of the neighborhood kids,
and although they all believe the story that Shane is guilty, none of them had any useful information that said he did it."

"And that's good?"

"Yeah, definitely good. It's just hearsay and rumor; even the witnesses who put Shane near the park have what I would call a weak recall. They couldn't identify or describe the other individuals who were supposed to be with Shane, even though they know Shane's best friends. They also had no idea what the individual they believed to be Shane was wearing; all they could say was that they knew it was Shane."

"Hmm? Do you think they're making it up? Do you think they're framing my Shane?"

"I wouldn't go so far as to say that, when people see things, or are a part of something bigger than themselves, oftentimes they talk themselves into believing things that aren't necessarily true, they create or buy into half-truths that have nothing to do with any facts or reality."

"Yeah, I can see that. Kinda like how the story gets better each time it's told until it becomes a completely different story."

"Exactly, you get it, and that's one of the things that makes our job so difficult, it's finding the needle of truth, in a haystack of bullshit, so how we are leaning is that it's very probable that these witnesses aren't necessarily lying, they are simply just wrong, and between the timestamp and the phone pings, we'll not only be able to cut Shane loose, but we'll be able to exonerate him completely."

"I'm so glad you're one of the good guys. I need my boy back and home, Tommy. I'm so glad you've stepped back into our lives and so glad you give a shit."

"I love you, Queens, always have and always will."

Queenie stood up and almost smiled, then hugged Tommy long and hard, "Fuck me, Tommy, where has the time gone? Was just yesterday we were Shane's age, running around outside like a band of gypsies. I miss those days."

"I do too, Queens, I do too."

She closed her eyes and kissed him again. "Now get outta here in case the FBI is taking my picture today." She said, once again, almost smiling.

Chapter Eleven

Tommy stepped out onto 1st Avenue and stood in front of Phil Hughes Pub, thinking about what to do with the rest of the evening. It wasn't yet 7:00 PM, and he wouldn't be on duty again until the next day's evening shift. He hesitated, then pulled out his phone and called Molly. There was no answer, so he sent a simple text message: "Are you working?" Then, he began walking south toward 85th Street.

When he hit 86th Street, his phone buzzed, "Hey, sexy man! Yes, I am. You coming over? I'll be done at 8!"

Tommy opened the door to Bailey's Corner and stood there as he did the other day, and watched Molly make her way up and down the bar for a moment.

She was dressed all in black, with a tight black babydoll tee, tight black jeans, and black Doc Martens. She turned, almost in slow motion, and Tommy caught her eye. As he did, a broad smile immediately appeared. As she always did, she rushed from behind the bar and ran to Tommy, jumping up into his arms for a tight embrace as she peppered his face with little mini kisses, then ran back to her place behind the bar.

He removed his blazer and hung it on the back of the chair. Before he sat down, he had a bottle of beer and a double shot of Jameson in front of him, and she was already pouring herself a shot of Shanky's Whip.

She picked up her glass and waited for Tommy to do the same, then clinked hers against his and tossed the shot down her throat before spinning around and attending to her waiting customers.

Tommy sat and watched her float around the bar like a beautiful butterfly from patron to patron, pollinating each with a smile, a joke, or a sarcastic remark, occasionally returning to him for the same, "What you think tonight, lover? Some sushi? Maybe Chinese?"

"Not feeling anything Asian tonight. How about we head over to the Mansion?"

"Ooh, yeah! Been a minute since I had a burger. Sure, let's do that."

A few more minutes passed, and Jack Norris, Molly's relief, came in and slapped Tommy on the back,

"Hey, how you been, Tommy? Good to see you, pal." He said as he walked by. Then, he and Molly did their thing and changed the register drawers as she counted her tips and made her way around the bar.

Sitting on the stool next to Tommy, she shouted, "Jackie, can we get one more round for me and my guy over here?" Jack poured Tommy another shot of Jameson and delivered a shot of Shanky's to his coworker, Molly.

She threw the drink down quickly, then wrapped her arms around one of Tommy's and leaned tightly into his shoulder, "What's up? I can tell something's bothering you."

"What you think, Molly?"

"It's that boy from the park, isn't it? I heard it was a bad one. Is it getting to you? – Do you think you need to talk to somebody, you know, you can always talk to me, Tommy, but maybe you should talk to a professional, you know, a therapist?"

"They all get to you a bit, Molly. Every case leaves its mark, but no, it's not so much him as it is the puzzle, the not knowing who did this or where to look… That's where the stress, my stress, comes from anyway, I hate not knowing and being helpless."

"Well for what it's worth, I know you're going to find whoever did this, you're one of the best, you see things and find things that no one else can, I know your job is hard, and hard on you, but I also know you will prevail, because you actually care, you care so much Tommy, I know you won't give up, and soon you'll have your man, just gotta stay strong and focused.

"Thanks, kid, I appreciate the kind words," Tommy did appreciate her kind words, but they did little to alleviate the troubles that were bouncing around his head at that moment.

"Come on," Molly said, "let's get outta here, grab a bite, and then I'll make you forget all about your cases and criminals."

The two made their way to the Mansion Diner, a block away on 86th Street. The place was busy, but they found a booth in the back. Molly ordered a cheeseburger and fries with a Coke, and Tommy a turkey club with sweet potato fries and an unsweetened iced tea.

"Listen, Molly, there's no way for me to make this gentle or easy. We've got to stop seeing one another."

The ever-present smile immediately left Molly's face, "Well, fuck me, Tommy, wow, talk about some blunt force trauma, I really didn't expect that... Wow, holy shit, that's a blow I didn't see coming."

"It's just wrong, honey. We are wrong together. I am way too old for you, and as much as I..." He paused and placed his hand on hers. "You are wasting your time with me, Molly. You should be spending your time with a younger man, finding someone you want to build a life with, and there is no way that can be me."

She pulled her hand away and sat silently for a moment, looked down at her burger then back up at him, "Listen, we've had this talk before, I'm a grown woman, and I know what I want, and let me break it to you there, charmer, I know, I know this thing we have, as beautiful and marvelous as it is, can't last, I don't picture ever walking down the aisle to meet you, or any kind of matrimonial bliss, but fuck me, Tommy, if I don't want you now... and if every moment we've spent together hasn't been magic."

"Listen, Molly..."

"No, wait, you listen. I know you're crazy about me; I know it because I can feel it, but I also know you are right. I do, I do, I actually think about it all the time, especially, oh god, especially after you got shot…"

"I just want…"

"No, let me finish, let me get this all out. Right now, today, you are the most amazing man I have ever met, but I know…" She paused as a tear ran down her cheek, and she wiped it away. "I know I could never make you my everything. I know you could never be my world, and I also know that in order for me to find someone else, I will have to quit you. I know, Tommy, alright, I know."

"So, we agree then?"

"Yeah," she wiped another tear from her eye, "Yeah, we fucking agree," they both sat for a second looking into one another's eyes, "But know I love you, you old motherfucker, you have been such an exciting roller coaster ride to be on, Tommy, but yeah, yeah we agree."

They then finished their meals in almost silence, until Molly began again, "Tomorrow you're on nights, yes?"

"Yes, I am."

"Okay, then listen, this is what we are going to do. Tonight, you're going to spend one last night with me, and then tomorrow, we're going to get up and go to Gracie Mews for breakfast. You're going to buy me blueberry pancakes, and then you and I are going to walk arm in arm up to the Met (Metropolitan Museum of Art), then after that we'll walk through Central Park and over to the zoo and look at all the animals and the birds, okay?"

"Oh, Molly, I don't know, I think…"

"No, I do know, that is exactly what we're going to do. I love you, Tommy, and I know you love me even if you don't say it, so we will have the sweetest breakup ever, one last perfect date. We are going to savor tonight and what we have of tomorrow as if you were some World War Two soldier being sent away to fight the Nazis, and it was our last day together before you leave. And then, well… I'll have to ask, please, after our last kiss, you don't come around Bailey's anymore, at least not while I'm working, okay? I don't think I could take it."

"Whatever you want, Molly, anything you want, I'm yours."

***

Molly closed the door to her bedroom and lit a single candle that sat on her nightstand. She walked over to him and slowly removed all of her clothes, and then she slowly removed all of his. While removing his pants, she remained on her knees, took him into her mouth, and worked her head up and down for a few minutes.

Molly then slowly and silently stood up and maneuvered Tommy over on the bed, lay him down on his back, and then straddled him, leaning over and kissing him deeply before sitting up and slowly inserting Tommy into herself, letting out a slight gasp before she began rotating her hips and gyrating in a slow rhythmic manner. As his body started to tense from the extreme pleasure he was feeling, she stopped.

"No-no, lover, do not finish. We are going to take our time tonight. You are in for some tantric shit, okay? Are you good?"

He nodded, and she began again. This went on for several minutes, Molly pausing every time she felt him start to enjoy it too much. She leaned down and kissed him as she placed her hands and arms behind his back and shoulder blades, then, leaning back, pulled him up into a sitting position and wrapped her legs around his waist, continuing to gyrate her hips ever so slowly.

"You, Tommy Keane, will never forget tonight and will never forget me. I will live in your heart and haunt you in your dreams for the rest of your life."

They remained entangled like this for almost twenty minutes, sweating face to face, kissing gently in between the sweet and sexy comments she would make, Tommy silent, nearly in a trance.

"Are you ready? Do you want to finish?"

Tommy nodded, and Molly stopped. She lay flat on her back, her head on the pillow, and her knees bent. Tommy climbed on top of her, looking into her eyes. Just as he re-entered her, she said, "You may finish, but please make it last as long as you can."

And he did. He lasted for several more minutes until the pleasure and exhaustion were too much to handle. As
he lay on top of Molly, both were more than satisfied, a single tear of sorrow ran down her cheek, and they fell fast asleep in one another's arms.

Chapter Twelve

The following morning, Tommy woke up to the cold feeling of the covers being pulled from his naked body, and then the sharp pain of a surprisingly hard slap on the ass as he lay in bed on his stomach.

"Get up! Get out of bed! We only have a few hours left, so don't waste them sleeping!"

Tommy rolled over and sat up.

"Come on, get up! We need to get in the shower, and have you bang me in there one last time before we go to breakfast!" Molly said, with a less-than-somber, almost jubilant attitude.

And that is exactly how they started their day, with another round of sex in a hot shower, after which they both got dressed, he in his work clothes from the
day before, charcoal slacks, a button-down shirt, and a muted plaid charcoal blazer.

Molly wore a crisp, tight white button-down shirt over a black bra, a short black pleated mini skirt, thigh-high stockings that allowed four inches of skin to show between them and the skirt, and high-heeled boots.

She looked spectacular, and Tommy said nothing more than "Wow" as Molly stepped out of the bedroom and said, "Are you ready, dear?"

Everything Molly wanted that day was delivered. She got her blueberry pancakes and spent an hour-plus at the Met, mostly in Gallery 548, the European Sculpture Gallery, which held many classic marble statues by artists like Rodin, Guidi, and Canova. This was Molly's favorite gallery in the Met, one of her favorite places in the world, and something she very much wanted to share with Tommy, here she explained the histories of several of the artists and their magnificent works to him.

After the museum, they enjoyed a long walk around Central Park and a trip to the zoo, where they watched the sea lions and penguins be fed, made their way through the hot, steamy tropics building, and saw every other exhibit the small zoo offered.

It was precisely what she hoped it would be - an almost perfect day.

They then returned to her building, where Molly stood one step above Tommy, at the top of her stoop, making her as tall as he was. They kissed one last soft, meaningful kiss.

With her beautiful green eyes staring deep into his, she said softly.

"I will love you forever and never forget you, Tommy," as a single tear ran down her cheek, then she turned and entered her building. He could see her through the glass as she made her way up the stairs and watched her until she was gone.

And then a single tear ran down his face.

Chapter Thirteen

Tommy had just enough time to get up to 88th Street, shower, shave, and dress before kissing his mother and rushing out the door to catch a cab on 2nd Avenue.

As he stepped into the Squad room, Charice Tate, the Squad's PAA (Police Administrative Assistant), was making her way out.

"Handsome, Detective Keane, Charice heard you was back early from vacation. Where you been hiding yourself, man? I haven't seen you all week. Here, give me a little sugar," She said as she leaned in and hugged Tommy, "Now get to work! You getting behind on your workload. I know you been away but you owe 5s on several of your open cases, and you ain't makin my main man Lieutenant Bricks look bad at COMPSTAT this month, you hear me?"

"Yes, ma'am, I'll get them done this week, Charice."

Tommy found Doreen, Clay, and Mark already sitting at their desks. Doreen and Clay were typing away, and Mark had his face behind a newspaper.

"Hey, Mr. Man, how you doing today?" Doreen asked.

"Tommy! Welcome back, my brother!"

"Hey, Clay … Doreen, how you guys doing?"

"Just peachy, thanks."

Mark dropped his paper enough to peek over the top. "I've been waiting for you, Tom. Are you ready to go?"

"Sure, but where? What's going on, where we going?

"You and I are going to run down to see Lidia Schwartz and get that kid 343'd (a 343 is a non-prosecution) and then hightail it up to the Bronx and bring that boy back home to his mother."

"No shit! Well, alright then. So, the phone records came in?"

"Yes, sir, they did, so unless this kid is a master criminal and had his phone going at home and someone playing games while he was out committing murders, he's not our man."

"Alright, well, there is some favorable news."

"It's not all good, Tom."

"How's that?"

"Well, we still have an open homicide, and you, my friend, have been assigned to help me out with it, so don't get ahead of yourself with the joy, because we got some work ahead of us now, and we've lost an entire week with the wrong kid."

***

4:46 PM Manhattan Criminal Courts Building. Office of ADA Lidia Schwartz

"So, we want to 343 young Mr. Shane Southerland for the homicide of Mr. Antonio Canales?" Lidia asked.

"Yes, Lidia, we do."

"Well, Mark, we know each other well enough, and you know I trust you enough to do whatever you ask basically, but please show and tell me why we're sure Mr. Southerland is not our man."

Mark began methodically explaining why he no longer wanted to seek prosecution for Shane.

"Okay, here we go. Point one: the fact that Shane's name was written in the victim's blood at the scene, and presumably by the victim, we believe to be very unlikely, if not impossible, to have been done by the victim himself."

"Point two: The bloody footprints found at the scene, although matching the size of our suspect, do not match the brand of sneaker he is known to wear."

"Point three, I have here a photograph of a time stamp from a game our suspect was playing during the approximate time of the attack. We recovered this game from his bedroom, approximately ten blocks from the crime scene. Our suspect, Shane Southerland, has no siblings and only lives with his middle-aged mother, so we don't believe anyone else was playing this game at the time of the homicide other than him."

"Point 4, here is a record I received from Mr. Southerland's cell phone company showing his phone's IMEI number ping location to be on the block in which he lives, and at no time during that entire day to be within at least a half a mile of the location where the homicide took place."

Lidia briefly glanced at the paperwork and photograph. "Works for me, 343 granted. Go get this kid. I can't imagine what he and his mother have been through this week."

***

Tommy and Mark got in their car and headed back uptown; Mark called Queenie Southerland to tell her they would pick her up on the way to freeing her son Shane.

"That Queenie Southerland is one hard broad," Mark exclaimed after hanging up with her.

"I can see that, but how so?" Tommy replied.

"Well, she's been so quiet and calm through all of this, kind of matter of fact about everything, and a moment ago when I told her we were coming to take her up to the Bronx and release her son, there was, well, zero emotion."

"Really? What she say?"

"She said, 'Good, I'll be waiting on the stoop for you.' And that was it, no excitement, relief, joy or anger, just a matter of fact, 'Good.' I don't know. If it were my wife or me in this situation, we'd be beyond relieved and jumping for joy, even if we were pissed over everything that happened."

"Hey, everybody handles things differently; I am certain she is both very happy and relieved to end this nightmare. And like you said, she's a tough broad; she's not going to wear her heart on her sleeve or show you any emotion. I'm guessing emotion isn't Queenie Southerland's style."

Tommy and Mark picked Queenie up. She was standing on her stoop, waiting as she had said she would.

Mark attempted to make small talk on the way up to Horizon, but for the most part, it was a quiet and somber ride. By the time they arrived, Shane was all set and ready to go. Mark signed a few documents, and then the four of them got back into the car and headed back down to the Southerland's building.

Mark explained to Shane and Queenie how and why the arrest was made and then how and why the District Attorney's office declined to prosecute. Queenie remained silent the entirety of the ride, and so did Shane, apart from repeating his claims of innocence right from the start.

"Yo, I told you, Detective Stein. I told you I had nothing to do with any of this, I even told you to check my game and check my phone, and look, you did, and bang, now you're driving me home after sticking me up in that shithole for five days. So, you know what? Sorry if I don't thank you for letting me out, alright? You shoulda maybe listened to what I was telling you from the beginning."

"I can't argue with any of that, Shane. All I can say is I'm sorry—I truly am—but you were our number one suspect at the time, and as such, it was my duty to arrest you as quickly as possible, and I did. But that's no excuse for what you and your mother went through, and I know that."

They arrived, and as Shane and Queenie exited the vehicle, Tommy got out, and Mark followed.

"Listen, before you two go upstairs, I want to tell you a couple things. First, Mark is a fine man, and he never would have put either of you through this if it wasn't what was called for at the time with the little information we had. Also, and more importantly… and get this in your heads, this is still an active homicide investigation. I want the both of you to stay cool and low-key, do not, I repeat, do not get involved in, or take part in, any of the gossip or bullshit that's going to surround this case, okay, it's important to stay cool and keep a low profile."

Tommy paused for a moment to emphasize his statement, then continued, "But also, you two are of this neighborhood, be smart, keep your ears open, and when you hear something that may have some juice, and I'm sure you will, don't do anything other than call Detective Stein or myself. Don't do anything stupid, don't say a word to anyone other than Stein or me, you got that? We will catch whoever killed Tony and whoever it was who tried to put the finger on you, Shane. Just be cool, be patient, and please don't get involved in anything that will get either of you in trouble."

Queenie put out her hand and shook Tommy's firmly, silently agreeing. Then she took two steps toward the curb where Mark stood and shook his hand firmly. Shane then followed his mother's lead and did the same.

They had an understanding.

Chapter Fourteen

The shift was almost half over,
and Tommy and Mark stopped by the Midnight Express Diner,
located at 1715 2nd Avenue, to grab a meal and discuss the
case.

They took a seat at a booth, and a young man in his
mid-twenties took their order. Tommy got bacon, egg, and
cheese on a bagel with unsweetened iced tea, and Mark got tuna
on rye with fries and a cup of coffee.

Tommy began, "So, where we gonna start here, pal? I
know it can be distracting having to change gears like this, but
I also know you're already deciding on how we're going to
approach this one, so please, let me know what you're
thinking."

"Ha, yes, the wheels have been turning inside this
hamster wheel I have in my head, and we have two approaches.
One that we have barely looked at is the CCTV. We have very
little video from the park, Gracie Mansion, or East End Avenue
and the surrounding area. What we have has shown us nothing
so far, but also, we were truly, I'm sorry to admit, completely
misguided with this Shane situation."

Mark took a sip of coffee, cleared his throat, and continued, "So there's that, the collection of as much video as we can find, and then there is the one plus to this Shane situation, and of course that's got to be obvious to you?"

"Yes, sir, painfully obvious. Whoever killed Antonio wanted us to look at Shane because they know Shane, and that will be our connection. It will most likely be someone from the neighborhood, and I'll also submit to you that it will most likely be another teenager. Sure, I could be wrong, but I'll bet you a meal it's going to be another teenager, one who has an axe to grind against both Antonio and Shane."

"I'm not a gambling man Tommy, but I'll call Bingo for you right now because this is exactly what I'm thinking and how I think we need to proceed. Also, in light of me believing in your hypothesis, I'll pay you in advance and pick up the check today."

***

They finished their meals, then headed back to the precinct and discussed how the investigation had fallen off track with Lieutenant Bricks, Sergeant Browne, Clay, and Doreen. After which, Lieutenant Bricks authorized three hours of overtime for each to go and scour East End Avenue between 83rd Street and 91st Street, in search of buildings and businesses that had cameras pointing towards all entrances and exits of the

park on the day and time in question, to which an
additional ten cameras, and videos were recovered and added to
the six they already had.

It was decided that the following evening's tour would
be all hands-on deck. They would view all ten of
the new videos in depth and return to and review the
original six videos in search of any new clues they could find.

And with that the squad signed out, Tommy, quite tired
from the previous long night, early morning, and full day spent
with Molly, coupled with the long tour he had just completed,
caught a cab and headed straight to his mother's place, where he
found she and JoJo had already gone to bed, probably hours
before.

Tommy cracked the door open to his mother's room to
let little JoJo out and take him for a quick walk. As he was
scratching at her door the moment Tommy entered the
apartment. Then, the two of them retired to Tommy's bed and
curled up tight together for the night.

Chapter Fifteen

Tommy's eyes opened to the sound of the rhythmic beginning of 'Don't Match' by The Obvious.

"Stupid ass," he said to himself, unhappy he hadn't turned the alarm off on his phone. JoJo, hearing both the phone and Tommy speak, was now fully awake, alert, and standing with his front two paws on Tommy's chest.

"Okay, buddy, just a minute, alright?" he said as he rolled out of bed and did his morning fifty pushups in the dark, then turned the light on and pulled on some sweatpants and a hoodie, stuffed his .38 Centennial five-shot into his pocket, and headed out the door with JoJo on his leash.

They stopped on the stoop, and both looked to the left and then to the right, scanning the block before they stepped down onto the sidewalk and began walking west towards 2nd Avenue.

About halfway up the street, Tommy stopped and reversed the course, and they walked east toward 1st Avenue, then down the following block to East End, and across and into Carl Schurz Park at 88th Street.

They meandered their way on the twisty paths to
the Peter Pan statue, the scene of the crime; this is where Tony
Canales had been beaten to death. Looking at the area, no one
would have known the horrors that had happened there just a
week before.

Tommy stood there, where he believed Tony's feet
would have been, as best he could remember from the
photographs, but looking down, there was nothing. The Parks
Department had cleaned up the scene.

Tommy looked up at the statue of Peter Pan, whose
eyes faced down right to where Tony's body had lain days
earlier, and he spoke out loud to the statue, as he had to the
frieze of Minerva, who witnessed the murder of Li Jun, just
months before.

"What use are you, Peter? You watched the whole thing
happen, and not a fucking word, you got nothing to say, do
you?"

Tommy and JoJo walked around the circular garden that
surrounded Peter and took a seat at one of the benches facing
the front of the statue. It was a beautiful morning. Dozens of
red and yellow tulips bloomed all around the bronze statue, and
it was like a picture postcard. 'Almost perfect,' he thought.

Tommy sat, thought, and watched as others walked past
for almost an hour. He and JoJo then began to head out. As
they did, he turned and said, "Thanks for nothin', pal," to Peter,
then exited the park.

On their way home, they stopped by Glasser's Bake
Shop, where Tommy picked up an assorted box of treats for his

mother and a brownie for himself, the corner of which he broke off and gave to JoJo as he ate the rest on the way back to 88th Street.

When he arrived home, he found his mother sitting in her recliner, watching the news, with a cup of coffee in one hand and a cigarette in the other. He presented her with the box of baked goods and kissed her on the head.

"Listen, lady, I'm going to go lie back down for about an hour or so; then I'd like to take you to lunch before I have to head in for work tonight, unless, of course, you already have plans."

"Oh yeah, Tommy, plans? Like I have a full dance card this week. No, I'm pretty sure I can fit you into my schedule today, Tommy." Maria Keane replied with that old school sarcasm she was known for, and he loved so much.

After his nap, Tommy showered, shaved, and dressed, and was happy to see his mother had also put on a casual but handsome outfit for their luncheon. Then, together, they left and walked down Second Avenue arm in arm to 85th Street and the Budapest Café. Tommy had given Maria her choice of restaurant, and this was her decision. It was a tiny café, with a pastry cabinet in the front and several small tables tightly packed towards the rear.

They took a seat, and when the waitress came, Maria refused her menu: "No, thank you, dear. I already know what I want."

Tommy said the same: "Yeah, we won't need menus, thanks." Maria ordered the Goulash Soup, and Tommy ordered the Stuffed Cabbage.

The two made small talk and reminisced over their meals, coffee, and dessert for an hour or more before walking back home arm in arm. Although his mother's condition was not great, Tommy could see she was holding her own against her terrible affliction and was able to have a meaningful conversation. Although she repeated names and occasionally paused, she seemed to be doing well.

She told him as they walked, "The worst thing about this, Tommy, is the unknown, Tommy, it's not the end I'm worried about, Tommy, it's how I'm going to get there, how much am I going to lose? Will I forget you eventually, Tommy? Will I forget your sister Kathleen, her children, or your beautiful Caitlyn Tommy? Will I, will I forget myself?"

Tommy placed his hand atop Maria's hand that was wrapped around his arm and turned his head to make eye contact with his mother, "I don't know, Ma, but I'll tell you what, I'm gonna be with you the whole way, okay? You won't do it alone, I promise you that."

"You're a fine boy, Tommy; you always were."

Chapter Sixteen

Tommy made it to work about fifteen minutes early, just as Detectives Keogh and Volpe were heading out of the squad room with a perp in cuffs and a case folder under Volpe's arm.

Next through the door was Sergeant Browne, "Afternoon, Tommy, I know you guys have that Canales case to work on, and I know you just had a week off, but please see if you can get me something, anything, on some of your older cases, alright."

"You got it, Sarge."

Doreen and Mark followed. They were followed by Clay and Lieutenant Bricks, who quickly held a meeting for everyone present concerning the Canales case.

"Alright, we have a mile or more of videos to watch tonight. Who's catching?

"I am, Lu," Clay answered.

"Okay, well, barring any heavy cases or emergencies, I want all four of you poring over videos. In the event something goes awry tonight, and I certainly hope it doesn't, I want Doyle to stay here with Stein and review these videos. I know I have you on as the number two for this case, Tommy, but Doreen has a knack for these things, so if that works for you, Mark, that's how I want it."

"Works for me, Lu."

"Very good, get to work! I want all these videos watched and rewatched tonight!"

With that, the four of them dug in and began painstakingly watching the videos that had been collected the night before from all the different buildings up and down East End Avenue that faced the park on the night of the Canales homicide.

Watching videos this way was significantly more difficult and time-consuming than most would think. Some were in black and white, others were full color, many were high resolution, but others were considerably rough and grainy. This, coupled with the fact that quite often the piece of evidence one would be looking for could easily be a second long within an hour of footage, or covered by a passing vehicle, or overexposed by the flash of a headlight, things that made diligent concentration, and a sharp eye for detail a must, something in which Doreen luckily had a knack for.

About two and a half hours into their tour, Doreen spoke up, "Mark, here, come here. I think I have something for you."

"What did you find?"

"Here, look here." They both studied a minute of grainy, black-and-white footage she had enlarged as large as possible on her computer screen before it became completely pixilated. "Can you tell? Are these your two witnesses, the two girls who saw the boys run from the park?"

The video showed what appeared to be two females, one tall and thin and one short and round, walking across East End Avenue towards the park from the southwest corner of 86th Street.

"It's hard to tell here, but it certainly could be. These two women definitely fit the height and weight difference between them. Let's find what other videos we have that feature the same intersection.

It took a little bit, but they were able to find another building on the other side of 86th Street that had an even better angle and image of the two women in question.

Doreen quickly enhanced and queued up the video.

"I do believe that's them," Mark stated flatly. "Hey, Tommy, come over here and tell me what you think."

Looking over Doreen's shoulder, Tommy joined them and said, "Yes, those are your witnesses."

It was a short video clip that showed what the detectives believed to be Iyana Franco and Stephanie McCrain stepping up off of East End Avenue and entering Carl Schurz Park at the 86th Street entrance.

"Okay, we've identified a time and a location. Let's see if we can find a corresponding camera now, something nearby that will show our perps leaving the park."

They quickly searched all the hard drives and matched up the addresses with a camera facing any reasonable line of sight the girls may have had of the boys leaving the park.

They watched and re-watched several videos that fit the criteria, but nothing. They could find nothing suspicious or that fit what Iyana and Stephanie had described or could have seen from their viewpoint from the intersection of 86th and East End Avenue.

Knowing investigations did not always go as planned or as hoped, and that their diligence was paramount in searching through these videos, the team returned to searching the rest of the footage they had acquired.

About forty minutes had passed. "Hey, I have something here." Clay said aloud, "Three young men leaving the park at 90th Street. Come look and see if this interests you."

Mark and Tommy hung over Clay's broad shoulders as he restarted the video. It was a decent-quality color video showing three teens walking out of the park at 90th Street and giving a useful shot of each of their faces as they passed the camera.

"This is interesting," Mark said. "It's the proper time frame, but quite a few minutes later, and great images, but no way the girls could have seen these boys from where they were on 86th Street. But that doesn't mean they aren't just out of sight and watching them right now as we watch this here?" he paused and continued, "Also, there are only three boys here, and none of them are Shane."

"Let's see what else we can find," Tommy said before returning to the screen and the video he was watching.

Another twenty minutes passed, and Doreen spoke again. "Here I have the two women leaving the park at the 84th Street exit, and it looks like it's…" It's sixteen minutes after entering."

Mark and Tommy again leaned over Doreen's shoulders. They watched, then rewatched, clearer images of what appeared to be Iyana Franco and Stephanie McCrain leaving the park at the 84th Street entrance.

Then the four returned to their viewing. "Here, I think I found your vic." Clay said excitedly, "Come see if this is your guy."

Mark and Tommy got up from their desks and went to stand behind Clay as he showed them a decent image of what they believed to be Antonio Canales crossing East End Avenue into the park at 87th Street.

Approximately thirty minutes later, Clay also discovered a video of the three young men who exited at 90th Street, entering the park at 88th Street about twenty minutes before Antonio's arrival.

The team then spent another hour reviewing more and more videos they had recovered, but in the end, they decided they may have found Antonio's killers. There was zero evidence that any of these three teens had anything to do with the killing. Still, the time frame was correct; what was unclear was the statements made by Iyana and Stephanie, who said they saw four boys leave the park, one of them being Shane.

"I don't get it." Mark began. "If these are our perps, they definitely line up timewise with the girls witnessing them leave the park, but they couldn't have seen them from 86th, much less 84th Street. Also, why would the only one they recognize or have a decent description of be Shane, who we can all see is not among the three we have on video?"

"Maybe the girls are just spreading rumors they heard? You know, making themselves a part of the story to gain attention?" Doreen asked.

"I can see that, but why drag Shane into it?"

"They must have heard Shane's name was written in blood on the pavement?" Doreen said.

"Plus, we know Stephanie didn't like Shane. She thought he was mean for making fun of her." Tommy added.

"That's true… looks like we're going to have to bring the girls in for longer, more in-depth interviews," Mark replied.

"Absolutely, but I think we'll need to identify and find these three young men before we do that. We've already released Shane, so if these three are indeed involved, they're already afraid the heat may have been turned up a bit now that Shane is no longer a suspect, and we don't need any of them disappearing on us," said Tommy.

"You're right, Tom. If the word gets out to these kids that we're trying to identify them, we may have difficulty finding them. The question is, who do we ask for an ID? The girls gave us nothing but Shane the first time around, so asking them again, I believe would be fruitless, and again if word gets out, which we know it would with these two, it might make locating these boys more difficult, and I hesitate asking Shane if he knows them because of his family ties."

Tommy knew exactly what Mark was saying, but wanted to ask and clarify, "What do you mean, Mark?"

"I mean," Mark paused, "With Shane's mother being who she is and having the connections she has… after her son was imprisoned for a week… If they find these kids before we do, we may have three more homicides on our hands than we do now."

It was late, their tour had ended, and the next day was the squad's RDO (Regular Day Off), so it was decided that Mark and Tommy would return for a day tour the next day and see if they could identify the three teens, they saw leaving the park.

Chapter Seventeen

Tommy awoke before the alarm on his phone sounded and rolled out of bed for his fifty morning pushups. He threw on some sweats and took little JoJo out for a quick walk. He showered, shaved, and got dressed for the day.

As he was unlocking the apartment door to leave, his mother emerged from her bedroom.

"I'm so glad I caught you before you left, Tommy. I waited up for you as long as I could, but I couldn't last, and I went to bed about a quarter to twelve last night, Tommy."

"Really, Ma? Why, what's up? You feeling alright? Come, come sit down in your chair." He replied, taking his mother by the arm and walking her toward her chair in the living area.

"Yeah, yeah, I'm fine, Tommy. I feel wonderful, dear. I wanted to talk to you, though, Tommy, about that boy from the park, that Spanish boy that got killed, Tommy. You're working on that case, aren't you, dear?"

"Yes, ma'am, I am. What would you like to know, Ma?"

"It's not what I want to know, Tommy.
I heard something you may want to know, Tommy."

Tommy became curious. "What you got? You hear something?"

"Yes, I did, Tommy. I heard that you police let that Shane Southerland go, that you let him free, no charges?"

Tommy replied, "Yeah, Ma, he wasn't involved in the murder; he was just a bad tip, and the witness had it wrong."

"That's what I heard. The girls, Bridey and Nora, said you grabbed the wrong boy. They think you should be looking for one of the Boyle boys and his friends, Tommy, you know, Cathy Boyle, maiden name was Mulvaney, she's like six years younger than you, so maybe you don't know her, Tommy?"

Tommy sat beside her on the sofa. "What did you hear, Ma?"

"The girls were saying that the new rumor is that one of the Boyle boys was the one who killed that Spanish boy. Said he and a few others beat him to death for no good reason, Tommy, but I don't know. You know how these girls gossip. A few days ago, it was the Southerland boy; now, it's the Boyle boy. Tommy, now is it true? I have no idea, but I wanted to pass it on to you, Tommy."

He leaned back on the sofa, and a slight grin appeared on his face, "Look at you, you and your little clutch of parish pigeons looking to right wrongs and solve crimes after communion."

Tommy leaned in and put his hand on his mother's knee, "You're the best, Ma. Thanks for waiting for me last night and for the information. You know to keep this to yourself and not tell anyone you mentioned this to me.

"Of course, Tommy, I would never mention it to anyone else."

"Good girl, I love you, Ma," he said as he stood and kissed her on the head, then headed out the door and off to the precinct.

'Imagine if this is true,' Tommy thought as he scanned the block from left to right and stepped off the stoop onto the sidewalk, 'Imagine my crazy old mother pointing us in the right direction to catch these killers, all because of some gossip she heard from two other old biddys she shares a pew with at mass?"

***

Tommy was the first to arrive at the precinct. He immediately sat down and began to run the name Boyle. He found several matching names and addresses in the neighborhood, including one Catherine, who lived on 89th Street.

As Mark walked into the Squad Room, Tommy looked up from the desk and grinned. He happily announced, "We've got our first lead for today here, Mark. Are you ready to hit the street?"

"Damn, Tom, you don't give a guy a chance to prepare for the day, do you?"

"C'mon, what do you need? A cup of stale coffee? To pick out one of the two old ass ties out of your briefcase? C'mon, I'll buy you some coffee along the way, and you can put your tie on in the car, or fuck it, go tieless today, live on the edge, will ya? We got a lead, and it's the first few minutes of the day. Let's go."

8:04 AM 220 East 89th Street

Mark and Tommy see the name "Boyle Apartment 2B" next to the bell in the vestibule. "What do you think? Do you want to ring it or have the super let us in? Tommy asked.

Before Mark could answer, a young woman of about twenty-five left the building. As she did, Tommy held the door she unlocked open, and Mark opened the door to the street for her. Then, both climbed the stairs to apartment 2B.

They stood silently for a moment. They could hear talking behind the door, so after nodding to Mark, Tommy knocked, and a young man answered,

"Who is it?"

"It's the police, detectives from the 21st Precinct." Open up, please."

"Okay, just a minute," the young man could be heard shouting, "Ma, the police is here."

"What? The police? What in god's name?"

The locks on the door began to tumble, and the door opened a crack. A woman of about forty with light brown hair looked through it over the chain that she had yet to release.

Tommy and Mark showed their detective shields to the woman, who shut the door, undid the chain, and reopened it completely.

"Good morning, Detectives. Is everything alright?"

"Good morning, Mrs. Boyle. It is Mrs. Boyle, yes?" Mark asked.

"Yes, yes, sir, it is." Catherine Boyle stood before them in a pink fleece zip-up robe and pink slippers, looking every bit the tired working-class woman she was, trying to get her two boys off to school before she headed off to work herself, where she would put in her eight hours as a case worker for the health care center on 95th street.

"Do you have a teenage son, Mrs. Boyle?"

"I have two. What, why? Have either of them done something I don't know about?"

"Are they home now? May we speak with them?"

"Yeah, both are heading out to school just now, is there, what? What is going on? Are they in any trouble?"

"We just need to ask them a few questions, Mrs. Boyle. They may…"

"They're here about Tony, Ma… Aren't you?" a tall, lean young man of about sixteen with dark hair, wearing a blue and grey rugby shirt and blue jeans, standing in the cased opening, leaving the kitchen to the living room, said.

"Yes, sir, we are," Mark answered.

"Tony, that boy that was killed in the park, you know something about that, Timmy?" Catherine Boyle asked, her voice cracking as she began to panic.

"No, not much, Ma, but why else would they be here?"

"Your son obviously knows why we're here. May we ask him some questions, Mrs. Boyle?"

Cathrine Boyle was flustered as the panic began to set in. Still, somehow, she got the feeling from the calm demeanor of her son and the equally calm demeanor of the detectives standing in her doorway that she might not have anything to worry about. She started to relax and regain her composure.

"Yes, yes, of course, I'm sorry. Please come in and have a seat, Timmy, you too, sit down and, and can I get you officers a cup of coffee or something?"

"Thank you, no ma'am, but please sit with us here," Mark asked, and the four of them sat at the kitchen table.

"With your permission, Mrs. Boyle, your son Timmy here seems to know why we're here and what we want to ask him about. Is it all right for us to have a conversation?"

"Yes, by all means, go ahead."

"Alright, Timmy. You know we're here to ask you about Antonio. Is there anything you'd like to tell us right off the bat?"

"Hmm, I don't know. I knew Tony; he was a friend, a cool guy. I heard you arrested Shane Southerland for his murder, but I also heard you let him go; the word is he had an alibi."

"That's correct. Shane spent almost a week in Horizon, but we found out it couldn't have been him, and now we're looking again for whoever it was that killed Antonio."

"Well, I can't tell you who did it, but I can tell you that I never thought it was Shane."

"Really? Why's that?"

"He's too cool, and kinda, well, he's kinda connected, and if he was mixed up in something like this, I don't think it would be so obviously him if that makes sense?"

"Connected?" Mark asked.

"Yeah, Shane, he knows people, you know, like gangsters."

"He's a thirteen-year-old boy?" Mark asked, probing for more information.

"Oh, Jesus, a thirteen-year-old boy mixed up in murder and with gangsters?" Catherine asked loudly.

"Yeah, Ma, Shane is for real, but overall, he's a pretty chill kid, smart, and not a troublemaker at all."

Mark and Tommy were beginning to get the impression that Timmy Boyle would not be the killer they were looking for. He seemed way too relaxed, forthcoming, and rather clueless to the trouble he may be in, to actually be one of the group they were looking for, as well as there being nothing appearance-wise that resembled the three teens they saw on video leaving the park the night before.

"So, let me ask you, Timmy," Tommy said, "Who do you think may have been involved in Tony's death?"

"I don't know, Detective, I don't. Tony was very popular. I mean, I can't think of anyone who didn't like him, much less anyone who would kill him. I mean, this is all so crazy; everyone is talking about it, and everyone is shocked."

"You said you had two teenage boys, didn't you, Mrs. Boyle?"

"Yes, sir. My other son, Robert, is in the other room, still dressing. Would you like to speak to him as well?

"Yes, ma'am, please."

"Timmy, get Bobby, please."

"Bobby!" Timmy yelled.

"I could have done that, Timmy! Now, go on and get up; get your brother." Catherine said in a rather annoyed tone.

A moment later, Timmy returned, his thirteen-year-old brother in tow —a small boy in a Yankees baseball T-shirt and a look of mischief in his eyes.

"Hello, Bobby, how are you? I'm Detective Stein, and this is Detective Keane."

"Ooh, the cops!"

"Do you also know Antonio Canales, Bobby?"

Bobby gave a long, drawn-out, "Yeeaah! We all know Tony; he's a cool guy!"

"Do you know, or have you heard any rumors about what happened to Tony?" Mark asked.

"Yeah, he got killed! Some guys jumped him in the park and beat his brains out!" Bobby answered excitedly.

"Bobby!" his mother said sternly, letting him know to calm it down.

Mark continued, "What have you heard, or do you know who might have done this?"

"I know everybody was saying Shane did it, was all over school, even teachers were saying it, but we never believed it, did we, Timmy?"

"No, we didn't," Timmy replied.

"It turns out we agree with both of you. We had to check him out, of course; that's our job, you know. But now we know, Shane didn't do it, and you can tell everyone at school he didn't and that you heard it from us."

"Can I tell the teachers that too?"

"Especially the teachers." Tommy answered, "Let me ask you, Bobby, is anyone in school or the neighborhood saying that anyone else may have done this to Tony?"

"No, everybody thinks it was Shane."

Mark looked at Catherine and asked, "Mrs. Boyle, we have photos of some people we think may be involved in this case." Do you think we could take the three of you to the precinct and see if either of your boys could put any names to the faces we have?"

"Well, I guess, but they do have school and will already be late, and I have work."

"We can give them each a note," Tommy answered, "And we can explain to your job just how important it was you missed a few hours."

"Okay, let me call my husband first and make sure it's okay with him, too."

Catherine picked up her phone and made the call, "Hey, Tim, listen, I got two detectives here... No, no, everything is alright. They want me to go with Timmy and Bobby to see if they recognize anyone from some photos of some suspects they have from Tony's murder... Okay, yes, I'll tell them. Okay, thanks, love you."

Catherine looked up from her phone.

"He says yes." The boys both let out an excited "Yess!" as she continued, "But Daddy says this is important, and you two are to treat it as serious as a heart attack, no fooling around. If you see someone you recognize, you say something, and if you don't, you say nothing; Daddy also wants you to know that he's proud of you either way and that it's not snitching. Tony was a fine boy and whoever did this needs to be caught."

"Sounds like a decent man, your husband," Tommy said.

"He is."

"What's he do for work?"

"Local 3 electrician."

"First-rate job, good for him."

9:58 AM 21ˢᵗ Precinct Squad Room.

Mark and Tommy walked Catherine and her boys into the precinct and up the stairs to the Squad Room. All three of them were wide-eyed and interested in the surroundings.

"None of us has ever been in a police station before," Catherine stated.

"Consider that a good thing," Tommy replied. "No one ever comes here for anything pleasant."

"True, very true," said Catherine.

"So, here's what we're going to do," Mark began. We're going to interview you two gentlemen separately, okay? We'll show one of you some images and see what you think, and then show the other. Once we do that, we'll have you both come together and compare notes, okay?"

And that's what they did. They sat Bobby in the interview room alone while Timmy and Catherine sat in front of Doreen's desk, and Mark played some of the footage of the three boys leaving the park.

"Do you recognize any of these boys?" Mark asked.

"Yeah, this one," Timmy pointed to the screen, "is Brenden Coyle and this one is Luke Summers. I don't know this one, but I have seen him around the neighborhood."

"How do you know them, and what can you tell me about them?"

"I know them from school and just from around; they're both kinda douchey, smoke a lot of weed, pop pills; I'd be surprised to hear they killed Tony, though."

"Why would that surprise you?"

"Neither are particularly gangster, and I mean Tony would destroy them in a fight, I don't know, they're both pretty douchey dudes, but I wouldn't guess them to be killers."

"Fair enough. Can you do us a favor, Timmy, and go into that room down the hallway and send your brother out?"

"Sure thing."

It was now Bobby's turn. Bobby, Catherine, Tommy, and Mark all watched the same footage Timmy had just seen, and without hesitation, young Bobby let the room know what he thought.

"This guy is Luke, and he's a complete dickhead!"

Catherine was going to correct him on his language, but under the circumstances, thought it was apropos and fitting.

"And this guy is also a major jerkoff, and his name is Brenden; his younger brother is a jerkoff, too; I hate those guys."

"So, Brenden Coyle has a brother?"

"Yeah, Casey, both are major jerkoffs."

'The Coyle boys. You were one letter off, Ma, but that's okay; you got us here anyway,' Tommy thought to himself.

"How about this guy?" Mark asked, pointing to the yet-to-be-identified third boy.

"They call him 'Gonz' for some reason; I don't know his real name. But he's a dickhead too."

"These boys' troublemakers?"

"I never seen em do anything wrong except for smoke weed. I know Luke always has a knife with him, but no, I never seen them doing anything actually wrong. Some graffiti sometimes, but no, honestly, they don't even talk tough; they're kind of, I don't know, stupid losers; I think Gonz might even be partly retarded, either that or completely burnt out."

"Do me a favor, Bobby, and go get your brother," Mark asked.

As the boys returned, Mark said, "You two did so great for us today. You truly helped us out, and I mean a lot. Can I ask you two if you know where any of these guys live?"

Timmy shook his head. "No, I'm sorry, I don't.

Bobby said, "I think Brendan lives on 90th, but I don't know which building it is."

"How about where they go to school?"

"Luke is still in Wagner, Brenden. I'm not sure." Timmy replied.

"Yeah, Luke and Gonz both go to Wagner, and Casey, Brenden's little brother, goes too, but I don't know about Brenden either."

"You guys have been great. Now listen, this is important. Okay, don't tell anyone you were here today. You men did the right thing by coming to help us, but no one needs to know about it. Okay, keep it to yourselves."

"Yes, sir, we understand," Timmy replied, and Bobby nodded along.

Catherine then said,

"Glad we could help, Detective Stein, Detective Keane, and we won't be needing a note. I don't think I want any of the teachers knowing we were here, either."

"Good thinking, Mrs. Boyle, and thanks again for helping us out," Tommy said as he shook her hand.

Chapter Eighteen

Mark and Tommy began to work feverishly to find the three teens the Boyle boys had identified after Cathy Boyle and her sons left the office.

The trick would be to locate and quickly and stealthily arrest each of the boys, hoping to prevent any one of them from being alerted to the fact that their comrades were being picked up.

Mark got on the computer and quickly located the Coyle residence on East 90th Street, while Tommy tried to get some extra manpower since the A team was busy with court and the processing of an arrest.

It was still early in the day, and the Anti-Crime team wouldn't be in for hours yet, so Tommy picked up the phone and called Sergeant Ruffalo, who was working at the front desk.

"Hey, Sarge, Keane from up the squad here. Who's patrol supervisor today? – Do you think he, or you, could spare two crackerjack officers for a few hours? We need a couple of sharp eyes to sit on an address in plain clothes while we scoop up a couple of perps. May also need an extra car for transport." – "Outstanding, you are the goods, man. Thanks, we appreciate the help."

"All taken care of?" Mark asked,

"Yes, sir, he's going to send us two of our favorites, Rios and McCartney; he's calling them in off their sector now. We'll get them out of the bag (uniform) and into some street clothes and set them up at the Coyle building, see if the kid is coming or going, and if he is, they can snatch him up for us, meanwhile you and I will beat feet over to Wagner Junior High, and hopefully pull Luke and Gonz out of class, have them transported back here, and then try and find our boy Brenden, if Rios and McCartney haven't already grabbed him for us."

"I like it," Mark replied.

About fifteen minutes passed, and Rios and McCartney came walking through the Squad Room door,

"Hey, Ruffalo said you had a job for us?" McCartney asked,

"Yes, we do," Tommy replied and explained the scenario. He gave each of the officers a still photo taken from the video that gave a favorable likeness of each of the teens they were looking for.

He pointed out and explained that Brenden Coyle was the individual who lived in the building, but if they were able to identify any of the three, they were to arrest them on the spot, and these kids may be armed.

Tommy told them to get into their street clothes and suggested that one of them sit on a stoop of an adjoining building. The other take a position further down the block or across the street, close enough to give chase but not so close as to raise any attention by looking like two cops waiting to grab someone.

Both nodded in agreement, thanked Tommy and Mark for the opportunity, and headed off to the locker room to change and get up to their stakeout.

Mark and Tommy then left the building in hopes of finding and arresting one or two of their suspects.

2:04 PM 220 East 76th Street Wagner JHS 167

Mark and Tommy entered through Wagner's red doors and checked in at the front desk. Officer Johnson, the school cop, sat with a school security guard, and they asked Johnson to join them.

They went to the office, found Miss Stefcheck, and explained the situation, saying they were there to pick up Luke Summers and the still unidentified Gonzo.

At first, Michelle Stefcheck was shocked, appalled, and a little defiant to the detectives' requests to pick up the boys, but that defensive attitude quickly dissipated as the reality of the situation took hold.

She became a bit light-headed and had to sit down. "Oh my god," she said as she sat in her chair behind her desk. "How could those boys do this? – How?"

Michelle Stefcheck quickly regained control of her emotions and, with almost vengeful authority, determined which classes and classrooms each boy was in.

Together, Tommy, Mark, and Johnson, with Miss Stefcheck leading the way, made their way to Luke Summers's social studies class. As they approached the door, this five-foot-two assistant principal took charge of the situation, asking the three policemen for one second so she could deliver Luke without disturbing the class.

Michelle paused at the door, took a deep breath, and straightened her cardigan. Then, she opened the door slightly, saying, "Hello, Mr. Brooks. May I see Lucas, please?"

"Of course, Miss Stefcheck," he answered before turning back to his class. "Lucas, go see Miss Stefcheck. It appears she needs to speak to you about something."

Luke Summers hopped out of his seat and calmly walked out the door to see Miss Stefcheck, with her back to the wall, standing across the hall from Mr. Brooks' classroom.

Just as he made eye contact with her and began to speak, "Yes, Miss…" Tommy forcefully grabbed him. He spun him around, forcing him hard into the hallway wall so fast he had no chance to realize or comprehend what was happening until it was over, and he was in custody.

Tommy cuffed him and patted him down, and while doing so, he recovered a small thumb flick knife with a four-inch blade and a box of Marlboro cigarettes containing six pre-rolled marijuana cigarettes and two dime bags of marijuana.

Miss Stefcheck looked at him in disgust
but remained quiet as Tommy, Mark, and Johnson whispered
something to each other. Luke remained completely silent; his
eyes glued to the floor.

Officer Johnson walked Luke to the front Desk and had
him sit while Miss Stefcheck led Mark and Tommy to the
special education class, where Marco 'Gonz' Gonzalez
sat doing a reading assignment.

Miss Stefcheck did exactly as she had before and asked
the teacher, Mrs. Dinhoffer, to have Marco come see her in the
hallway. All went exactly as planned, apart from Marco being
considerably more upset than Luke was. Marco immediately
started crying aloud, asking repeatedly for his mother
and crying out, "Why are you doing this to me?"

The four of them made their way down to the school's
office, where Mark and Miss Stefcheck had Marco sit in a
chair. Tommy went to the front desk to check on Luke and
Officer Johnson, who informed Tommy as he arrived that
a patrol car had arrived to help transport one of the teens to
the precinct so they could keep them separated.

As Tommy and Johnson put Luke into
the patrol car and Tommy instructed the officers on what to do
with him, Mark and Miss Stefcheck notified both boys' parents
through their emergency contact info that they had been
arrested and to meet with Detective Stein at the 2-1 precinct.

Tommy and Mark then left the school with Marco and
drove him to the precinct.

Chapter Nineteen

Officer Rios sat on the stoop of 248 East 90th Street, a red brick five-story, ten-family building that sat just east of 246, another old brick tenement painted a cream color, which was Brenden Coyle's residence.

Officer McCartney stood directly across the street inside the black iron gate of Rupert Park, both quietly keeping their eyes open and scanning the block up and down, occasionally communicating via their cell phones to one another rather than their radios so as not to show themselves as police.

At 3:34 PM, Mark and Tommy arrived on the block. They had Luke and Marco being babysat in the interview room and muster room while they headed up to see if they would/could find Brenden.
Seeing both Rios and McCartney where they had stationed themselves, they nodded for Rios to join them inside the park across the street from Brenden's building.

The decision was made that Rios and McCartney would stay exactly where they had been and keep a lookout, while Mark and Tommy went to see if anyone was home at the Coyle residence.

Tommy and Mark easily gained entrance by ringing the bells to the two 5th-floor apartments, and someone simply buzzed them in. They then made their way up to the 3rd floor and apartment 3A, where they knocked on the door. While knocking a second time, they heard a woman's voice answer.

"Who is it?"

"Police, ma'am. We're detectives from the 21st precinct. May we speak with you, please?" Mark said as he raised his shield to the peephole.

The locks began to tumble, and the door opened to an older woman of about seventy, with long white hair done up in a bun on top of her head. She was wearing a blue housedress and fluffy blue slippers.

"What can I do for you, gentleman?" the woman asked in a kind and calm manner, seeming happy for the attention.

"Mrs. Coyle?" Mark asked,

"No, I'm Mrs. Fennessey, Mrs. Coyle would be my daughter, but she's not here right now."

"Okay, Mrs. Fennessey, are either of your grandsons home, in particular, Brenden?"

"Why no, no sir, but…" And before Mrs. Fennessey could continue, a voice came yelling over the radio,

"Foot pursuit, westbound on East 90th, male white, six-foot, black hair, denim jacket, headed towards 3rd Avenue."

Tommy and Mark made eye contact and ran down the stairs, out into the street, and headed
toward Third Avenue without saying a word.

They stopped when they could see Rios, McCartney, and whoever they were chasing were already out of sight, so they headed back to their car and pulled out, waiting for the next radio transmission.

Rios, who had been sitting on the same stoop he had before, saw Brenden walking down
the street from Third Avenue and gave McCartney a heads-up. McCartney moved up the block a few car lengths
and began to cross 90th Street as Brenden approached
his building, and Rios stood and began walking towards Brenden's building.

It was perfectly timed, but just
as Rios and McCartney stopped Brenden in front of
his stoop, Brenden took off like a shot, jumped onto, and ran over the hood of the car parked directly in front of his building, creating enough of an obstacle to give him a head start up the street with both McCartney and Rios behind him.

"Perp is southbound on 3rd Avenue, central!" came over the radio Rios' voice screaming and panting into his
keyed radio.

Tommy, hitting the gas, screeched through the red light, horns honking at him, then quickly turned up 89th Street and drove as quickly as he could toward 3rd Avenue. In the distance, they could see Brendan,
then McCartney, then Rios cross 89th Street.

As Brenden approached the corner of 88th and 3rd, a man stepped out of the door of Wankel's Hardware store right into the oncoming Brenden, knocking both to the pavement.

As Brenden quickly recovered from his fall, McCartney jumped on him and struck him several times into submission with his fist, then he and Rios cuffed him and all three sat on the sidewalk catching their breath.

Tommy pulled up in the bus stop going in the opposite direction of the 3rd Avenue traffic, cars honking at him and a cabbie cursing at him, "Wrong way asshole!"

Chapter Twenty

Back in the Squad Room, spirits were high. Mark and Tommy, along with the help of Patrol Officers Rios and McCartney, were able to nab all three suspects in the unbelievably heinous murder of Antonio Canales, all within a two-hour time frame and with no serious injuries other than a few bruises on Brendan Coyle.

Notifications had been made to both Luke Summers' and Marco Gonzalez' families at the school, and Mark immediately put a call into Mrs. Fennessey, Brenden's grandmother, to let her know her grandson was now in custody.

He also put a call into ADA Lidia Schwartz, who said she would make it up to the precinct for the interviews. Finally, he also notified Lieutenant Bricks of all that had transpired and exactly where they were with the case and the arrests.

Now came the waiting game, as all three perpetrators were minors, Mark and Tommy would have to wait for their parents or guardians to arrive before they could conduct any interviews. They would also wait for Lidia as she said she wanted to observe the interviews herself, and they also may have to wait on any counsel that may show up on the boy's behalf.

Mark and Tommy had a long night ahead of them, and they knew it, so Tommy ran around the corner to Niel's Coffee Shop and grabbed some sandwiches: A pastrami and rye for Mark, a turkey club for himself, as well as two burgers for Rios and McCartney, who they decided to keep on for the night to help with the babysitting of the three, as well as transport, and to answer questions from and give statements to ADA Schwartz, should she need them.

Mark and Tommy were about halfway through their sandwiches when Lidia Schwartz came walking into the Squad Room and set up shop at Doreen Doyle's desk,

"Don't let me interrupt you, gentleman, please, take your time, I have a feeling we'll be at this for a while tonight.

Next, at 5:48, Mrs. Mary Summers was escorted into the Squad Room by Officer Ortiz. Mary Summers was a short, thin woman of forty-two. There was nothing about this woman that stood out; she was as average as any woman could be. She appeared to be her age; she had long brown hair with threads of grey running throughout, mom jeans, running shoes, and a grey zip-up hoodie on. The only thing that made her stand out at this moment was the fear in her watery brown eyes, and the look of stress on her face.

Mary Summers was exactly what she appeared to be, an unremarkable working stiff who put in her forty-plus hours a week. She struggled to get by raising two children alone in a city that had become way too expensive for a simple hospital clerk in her situation to survive in, but also lacked the resources or dreams to leave in search of a better life outside of the only neighborhood and existence she had ever known.

Mark and Tommy stood to greet her.

"What happened, why do you have my Luke? Where is he, what? What has he done?" she frantically asked, tears running down her face and her hands trembling.

Tommy pulled up a seat and had her sit down, while Mark explained how he was believed to be part of the group who beat Antonio Canales to death.

She sat silently for a moment in disbelief, "No, no I know about this story, and no, there must be a mistake, my Luke couldn't have done this, it's not, it's simply not possible, I, I can't, I won't, I don't believe it, there has to be a mistake."

"Well, Mrs. Summers," Mark began, "We have yet to interview Luke, that's why you're here, but one thing I want you to know is that there is no mistake that he was in the park with two other boys on the night of, and the time, that Antonio was murdered, and we have him on video. So, when we sit down with him and you speak to him, it is imperative that you express to him that he needs to be one hundred percent honest. We know he was there, we know he was with other boys, and we know it was exactly when Antonio Canales was beaten to death."

Mark paused and let everything he had said sink in, "Now, please prepare yourself. When you're ready, we'd like to ask your son some questions. You will be right there with us while I conduct this interview, we just need to get to the facts,

Mrs. Summers, and Luke has a lot of questions to answer, do you understand?"

"Yes," she answered, taking a deep breath and wiping her eyes, she sat up straight and pulled her grey sweatshirt down a bit in an attempt to steel herself against the most frightening situation she had ever been in during her unbelievably boring, and average life; other than the day her husband had left her with two children and an empty bank account eight years before.

"I'm ready," she said.

Mark escorted her to the Box (the interview room) and sat her down at the table, and Tommy retrieved young Lucas Summers from the admin sergeant's office, where he sat with Officer McCartney. Together, they walked him into the interview room, where Mrs. Summers immediately sprang up from her seat, and threw her arms around her son, "Oh my god," she said aloud as she embraced him and hugged him with all her might, tears rolling down her face.

Luke hugged her back, but with much less intent or commitment than his mother hugged him,

"C'mon, Mom, you're embarrassing me," he said softly to her, "Stop cryin, will ya?"

"Listen to me, Luke," she said softly, but firmly, pulling back and holding him by the shoulders, staring intently into his eyes, "You tell these detectives the truth, and tell them, you tell them you had nothing to do with this, Luke, you hear me."

Tommy motioned for Luke and his mother to take their seats, and Mark read them Luke's Miranda warnings, and had them sign a piece of paper recognizing they had received them.

"Luke, you know why you're here, before we begin, what I want you to know is that we have video of you, and your friends Brenden and Gonz, we know where you were and we know what the three of you did to Tony, what we want to know is why?"

Luke fiddled with his fingers, his eyes locked on them as his hands rested on the table that separated him and Detective Stein. He said nothing, just stared at his hands, as his fingers nervously played with one another.

"Lucas, answer the Officer, answer him."

"I got nothin to say, Ma."

A look of fear took over Mary Summers face, "Lucas, you tell Detective Stien you had nothing to do with this right now, do you hear me…"

"Ma," he said looking into her eyes, and placing his left hand onto her forearm as a single tear appeared and ran down his cheek, "I need a lawyer, Ma, I, I can't talk without a lawyer, Ma."

Although Lidia, who watched from the observation room alongside Officer McCartney, would have rather had a full confession, or had Mark and Tommy work their magic and had Luke give them an incriminating statement, she smiled.

She smiled a broad smile to herself because what she had just witnessed was enough for her to know they had one of

Antonio's killers, and she knew in her heart that it was only a matter of time and going through the motions before these three teens would be convicted.

It was almost 7:00 before they sat Brenden Coyle and his mother, Theresa Coyle, in the Box. Theresa stood five feet six and weighed close to 200 pounds. She had shoulder-length jet black hair, a round red face that sat on a thick neck and broad shoulders. She was dressed in a black velvet tracksuit with white trim and was nowhere near as soft-spoken as Mrs. Summers was.

"Is this being recorded?" she asked in a rough and demanding tone.

"Yes, ma'am, it is," Mark replied.

"Good, good, I want it on tape, I want this recorded," she said, looking up into the corner of the room where the camera was visible, "Look, look at my boy's face." She grabbed Brenden's face and turned it, showing the bruise on his left cheek, "Here, where they beat my son, look at his elbow," she continued lifting Brenden's arm and showing where his elbow was scrapped from hitting the pavement in front of Wankel's Hardware store, "And here, here, look at the bruises on his back and his ribs," Lifting Brenden's t-shirt to show his injuries, "Again, where the police beat him, trying to get a confession from my son, they beat this sixteen year old boy - grown men, beating a young boy to get a confession for a crime he didn't commit!"

"Please, Mrs. Coyle, take a seat." Mark calmly asked.

"Or what? You'll beat me too, Detective Stein? No, no I will not take a seat, and we will not succumb to your threats or intimidation! My son is innocent of all charges, and we will not only not be talking to you today without a lawyer, but my lawyer will be suing both you and the city for millions over this false arrest, and the physical and mental abuse you have caused today!"

Theresa Coyle continued her ranting all the way down the stairs and into the street as she was escorted out.

Lidia again smiled. No, she wasn't getting any information, but she had gained insight into who she would be prosecuting and gained greater confidence that they indeed had the right perpetrators in custody.

As Theresa Coyle exited the building, still screaming like a banshee, Hector and Anita Gonzalez, Marco's parents, waited patiently on the stone bench that sat inside the doors of the precinct's lobby.

They were both escorted upstairs to the Squad Room by Officer Ortiz, then were seated in the Box. When Marco was brought to them, they immediately all embraced. Anita Gonzalez began to weep in disbelief at the experience she was going through.

The Gonzalez family was a decent, hard-working family. Hector was a plasterer who earned a respectable living with his trade, and Anita a home health care licensed practical nurse, who also made a decent living, and together they raised three children whom they absolutely adored, especially the youngest, their special needs child, Marco, who to them was an angel who could do no wrong.

They all sat where they were directed, and Mark and Tommy also took their seats. As they began, Mark made the introductions, being as pleasant as possible. Anita couldn't stop crying, and as Mark read Marco, and his parents, his rights, her sobbing became stronger, until Hector asked if it was okay if she could be excused, and "Only the men could talk." Anita was excused and took a seat in the Squad Room where Officer Ortiz got her a cup of coffee.

The interview began, and Mark calmly told Marco and Hector why they were all sitting there,

"Marco, please son, all we want is your side of the story, we know what happened to Tony, and we know you were there with Brenden and Lucas, we have video of all three of you," he placed the still photo they had taken from the video of the three teens where each of their faces were perfectly clear and undeniable.

Hector let out a distressing sigh of disbelief, which was filled with such deep sorrow that both Mark and Tommy felt for him, and even Lidia and McCartney were saddened from inside the observation room.

Tears ran down both Hector's and Marco's cheeks, and Hector leaned in and nodded his head slightly to Marco,

"Tell the truth, son, your mother and I will forgive you, and more importantly God will forgive you too if you tell the truth."

Marco took a very deep breath, "I love you, Poppi," then he slowly began to tell the story, "We went to the park to wait for him."

Mark interrupted, "Who went to the park and who did you wait for, Marco?"

"Sorry, sir. Me and Brenden and Luke, did. We went to the park and waited for Tony, and well, Brenden had put a bat and a stick in the bushes earlier, so we had a stash there waiting for us, and we waited on the bridge, you know where the statue is, you know where that's at, right?"

"Yes, Marco, we do."

"Right, so yeah, we waited for him and then he came, right. And well, so we did what we went there to do, and we jumped Tony. We all hit him with the sticks and the bat until he fell down you know like he was asleep, you know, not conscious."

"And what else? What happened next?"

Marco crying throughout his confession took a big deep breath and continued, "And then Brenden got this big rock, this big square rock from behind one of the benches and he, he, he made me take it and he made me throw it, he made me throw the rock onto Tony's head, and he, he told me I had to do it right or he was going to beat my ass if we had to do it more than once so I, I did it, I put the rock up high over my head and threw it as hard as I could onto Tony's head."

Mark reached across the table and placed his hand on Marco's arm, "It's alright, son, you're doing the right thing."

"Did you see Tony write anything in his own blood?" Tommy then asked.

"Nah, that …" Marco took a deep swallow and a deep breath, then wiped his eyes and looking at Tommy replied, "That was Brenden, he done that, he wrote Shane's name with Tony's finger and Tony's blood."

The whole room paused for a moment. The case was made, but Mark still had a question: "Why? Why did you boys do this to Tony? What did he do to make you hate him so much?"

"It was the girl," Marco answered.

"What? Was Tony chasing one of your girl friends?" Thinking it must be the ever-common love triangle that came to an end with Tony's murder."

"Nah, it was like a hit. She wanted him dead, she wanted Tony dead, and she wanted Shane to go down for it."

Mark and Tommy both remained silent for a moment, slightly shocked at what Marco had said.

"A hit? A girl hired you to kill Tony? And the three of you did? Who, who is this girl?"

Marco paused momentarily, and his father gently placed his hand on the back of his neck to comfort him. "It was Rotunda; she set it up and had us do it. I was scared and didn't want to do it, but Brenden said I had to, said I already took the payment, now I had to, and if I didn't, they'd beat my ass, so I, so I went along with it."

"How much did she pay you to kill Tony?" Mark asked in a lower tone.

"She, she didn't…" Marco paused and looked at his father in shame and disgust, but Hector looked back at his son with love and said,

"It's okay, son, go ahead."

"Nah, no money, she, she, they sucked us off, they sucked us off to get us to go do it and then owed us another one once it was over."

"Okay, so you, Brenden, and Luke received oral sex, blowjobs, in payment to kill Tony?"

"Yes, sir, Mr. Detective, that's how it happened."

"And you said they, Marco?" Tommy asked. "This girl called Rotunda? And who else?"

"Shadoof."

Chapter Twenty-One

Approximately ninety minutes had passed
since Mark and Tommy had concluded their interview
with Marco and Hector. Although miles of paperwork and
processing still needed to be done with these three young men,
it had all been put on hold for a moment so they could tie up
two loose ends.

10:12 PM

Detective Mark Stein and Detective Hernandez from
the C Team knocked on the door of one Iyana Franco.
Lucia Franco opened the apartment door.

"Sorry to bother you so late, Mrs. Franco, but we have a
development in the Antonio Canales case, and we
need Iyana and you to come to the precinct with us for a
statement, please."

"Seriously? Again? This can't wait until tomorrow?"

"No, ma'am, I'm sorry it can't, but it shouldn't be long."

10:16 PM

Detective Tommy Keane, along with Detective Kevin
Reardon of the C Team, knocked

on Stephanie McCrain's apartment door. Stephanie, recognizing Tommy through the peephole, opened the door to him.

"Hey, Stephanie, how you doing? Is your mom home?"

Stephanie smiled, "Hi, Detective Keane. Yes, one minute. " Then she yelled, "Ma, it's the police."

Mary Ann McCraine came to the door. "Sorry, I know it's getting late, but we have to bring you two in for another statement regarding the Tony Canales case. It shouldn't be too long, Mrs. McCrain."

"Really? She said, somewhat annoyed, okay, I guess if you need us, we have to go… Stephanie, grab a jacket or a sweater."

10:46 The Box

Mark and Tommy sat down with Iyana and Lucia Franco, and Mark read Iyana and her mother Iyana's rights.

"Wait, what is this? What exactly is going on here?" Lucia Franco asks in a terrified and concerned voice, realizing something had changed with the case.

Mark continued, "Iyana, you are being charged in the murder of one Antonio Canales…"

Iyana immediately interrupted, "Ha, I didn't murder nobody; I had nothing to do with that at all. It was Shane, Shane Southerland, that done that!"

"No. No, Iyana, it wasn't Shane Southerland; it was you. We picked up Brenden, Gonz, and Luke a few hours ago, and we know everything that happened, and we know you were involved."

"Lies!" She shouted, "Those boys are all liars. I, we, we saw them there, alright, we saw them in the park, and we saw what they did, and they threatened us. They said they'd kill us too if we snitched, and told us to say Shane done it, that's right, that's it, they said they'd kill us if we didn't tell you that we saw Shane in the park."

"Shut up! Shut your fucking mouth!" Lucia interjected, slapping her daughter Iyana across the face, "No more, not another word. Do you hear me, you stupid, stupid bitch!"

Then, turning to Mark, brushing her hair back from her face and lowering her voice, she started over: "We're done here until we speak to our lawyer, Detective Stein."

11:28 PM The Box

Mark and Tommy sat down with Stephanie McCrain and her mother, Mary Ann, and Mark read Stephanie her rights.

"Hold on, what in the world is happening here, Detective Stein? What in the world is happening?"

"Stephanie, you are being arrested for the murder of one Antonio Canales."

"How is this possible, Stephanie?" Mary Ann asked her daughter, "What in the world?"

Stephanie looked at her mother. "I'm sorry, Mommy. I didn't do it, I swear, I was just there, I swear, I swear it, I didn't hurt Tony, I swear, it was all Iyana and those boys, I was, I was just there."

"Oh my god! Stephanie, darling, what did you do? How ...how did you get mixed up in this?"

"It wasn't me, Mommy," Stephanie reached out and took both her mother's hands in between her own, and with eyes that pleaded to be believed, she began, "It was Iyana, Mommy. She was trying to get Tony to like her, and she, well, she gave him, oh God, she gave him a blowjob in the bathroom of the pizzeria. And, well, he still didn't like her, and even worse, he told everyone and made fun of her for being, you know, overweight. He also said she couldn't do it right."

"Do what right?" Mark asked,

"You know, do blowjobs, said she was not good, told everyone she sucked and sucking."

"So, she decided to kill him?" Mark asked.

"Yeah. Yes, sir, she, well, she couldn't do it herself so she got those boys to do it, she set it all up, she planned the whole thing with them and then messaged Tony that afternoon and told him to come to the park and that she would BJ him again, that he would know what a first-rate one was when she was done with him."

"How did she get the boys to do it?"

Stephanie paused, she stared down at the table for a moment, then said through tears, "I'm sorry, Mommy, I'm so, so sorry," then, directing her answer to Mark, continued, "She had me and her BJ the boys for payment." Mary Ann hung her head in disbelief. "She, Iyana, BJ'd Brenden, and Gonz, and she made me BJ Luke. I didn't want to, I swear; I didn't want anything to do with this."

"Were you there? We have you on video entering and leaving the park that night."

"Yes, yes, we watched, oh my god we watched and were lookouts from up on the bridge, and
the boys just beat and beat him, they beat him, and he
went right down and barely even yelled out, he dropped to the floor, but they kept hitting him again and again."

"What happened with the rock, Stephanie?"

"Oh god, that was the worst part, so Brenden gets this big rock right, and gives it to Gonz, and tells him to drop it on Tony's head, says some mean stuff to him, like he's gonna be next if he doesn't do like he's told."

Stephanie paused. She had gone completely white. She took a deep breath and regained her composure. "And then he did it, he did what Brenden told him. The sound—I can't stop hearing it—the sound of that rock hitting him."

"And once it was all over?"

"Well, we went home to Iyana's place, and then the next day, the next day, we all met up, you know, and we, sorry, Mommy, Iyana BJ'd Brenden, and I BJ'd Luke. Then we all planned to play it cool, and that was that."

"And Gonz? Who took care of Gonz?"

"No one. He didn't want anything to do with anyone for the next few days, but I think Brenden got to him and got him to stop being a pussy about it… Sorry, Mommy."

"And why Shane? Why did you pull his name into this?"

"They wanted you to go after him."

"Why?"

"Because we, we hated Shane,"

"Why?"

"Shane thought he was so cool. You know, he's like connected and untouchable around the neighborhood, and he thinks he's real funny and makes nicknames for everybody, and well, like with Gonz … Yes, his last name is Gonzalez, but we all call him Gonz cause he's special ed. His brain is Gonz, and me, he named me Shadoof, because he thinks I'm a doofus and because I'm a girl, so like she-doof, and now the whole neighborhood, and everyone at school knows me as Shadoof, and Iyana he nicknamed Rotunda, because she's short and fat, which I think means rotund? But also, sometimes just Tunda, which means thunder thighs, and she hates it, so she decided to kill Tony for what he did and put Shane away for what he did."

"And how are you feeling about this, Stephanie?"

"Oh my god, I hate it all so much, I didn't want to be in this, but Iyana made me, and Brenden was all mean and scary, and it really is the worst thing ever. Tony didn't deserve this at all. He wasn't a bad person, and even though
I hate him, Shane isn't bad either. He ... he actually stood up for me once." She paused and swallowed. "Some kids from uptown was getting kinda handsy, and was pushing me around, and you know, touching me places. Shane and his boys ran over and threatened them, and then they walked me home, which was sweet and kind I guess, but then when I thanked them, they still called me Shadoof after, so I don't know what to think
of Shane, to be honest."

***

Once all the interviews were completed, Mark and Tommy, with the help of Officers Rios and McCartney, processed all five teens and then transported and lodged them all at Horizon, the same place the five of them sent Shane.

Lidia wrote up the cases that evening, and, aside from the numerous upcoming court proceedings, the Antonio Canales case was closed.

And around 3:00 AM, they all said their goodnights and made their way home.

Tommy was broken and tired from the week and the double shift he had just worked. He caught a cab uptown, hoping to grab a beer and a shot before he made it home to his mother.

But instead of taking the cab to his usual haunt, Bailey's Corner on 85th and York, he had the driver take him to 85th and 1st, and he walked into another old neighborhood landmark, the Ryan's Daughter Pub, a place he was very familiar with but hadn't frequented for years.

An attractive young woman in her mid to late twenties, wearing a snug-fitting T-shirt and tight jeans with a long brown ponytail, was behind the bar.

She tossed a coaster his way. "You look like a cop," she said.

Tommy nodded.

"What'll it be, Officer?"

"Give me a bottle of Bud and a double of Jameson, please."

The woman walked down the bar and returned, placing the bottle of beer on the coaster, a rocks glass, and a shot glass in front of Tommy. "Looks like you had a long day today, am I right?"

"It's been a long week." He replied as she filled the rocks glass and then the shot glass.

"My name's Jenna, and this rounds on me," she said, raising her glass. Tommy raised his, and as their glasses clinked, he replied, "Thanks, Jenna. I'm Tommy. It's nice to know you."

Jenna smiled, "Know me? - You don't know me… Not yet anyway." She replied with a wink and a coy smile as she turned and walked back down the bar to attend to the rest of her customers.

Epilogue

Stephanie McCraine agreed to testify in court against all the others in return for a sentence of no jail time and ten years' probation.

In the end, only one case went to trial, that of Brenden Coyle.

Lucas Summers went through all the hearings and motions right up to the day his trial was to begin, when his counsel got him and his family to relent and take a plea. He received seven years for the part he took in the Antonio Canales homicide.

Marco 'Gonz' Gonzalez, along with his family's support, immediately pled guilty to the part he played in the homicide.

Due to his low IQ, and letters from his school, his church, and the testimony of Stephanie McCraine, who said she knew he was coerced into crushing the skull of Antonio Canales, by the threats made to him by Brenden Coyle, the judge ordered him into a minimum security youth facility in upstate New York until the time of his 21st Birthday and under the condition he graduate high school, after which a ten year probation sentence would commence.

Antonio Canales

Iyana Franco did not plead guilty at first to her part in
the murder. Her defense was that she was the victim
of both Brenden Coyle and Antonio Canales, claiming
that both would regularly sexually abuse her and that she lived
in fear for her life.

However, after the courts admitted into evidence the
cell phone records of all parties involved provided by the
District Attorney's Office, it was obvious that Iyana not only
concocted the plan to murder Antonio but lured him to the
park that evening with a promise of oral sex.

She also offered up sexual favors as compensation
by both her and the unwilling Stephanie McCraine to the male
actors in this conspiracy and nowhere was there
any evidence found of any physical or sexual abuse
towards Iyana by Antonio Canales or Brenden Coyle.

The judge in her case decided to sentence her as
a youthful offender rather than an adult and sentenced her to
eight to twelve years rather than fifteen to life.

Brenden Coyle was also sentenced as
a youthful offender by the judge who cited the fact that
although he may have been the leader of the three youths who
committed the crime, he was not the one who planned or
orchestrated the attack.

It was also unknown exactly what weapon or which
individual among the three struck the killing blow, as it was
argued Antonio may have already been dead before him being
hit in the head with the Belgium Block, according to testimony
made by each of the defendant's counsel.

For his part, Brenden Coyle received a sentence of ten to fourteen years.

Shane's attorney sued the City of New York for false arrest and imprisonment, and although it took eight years to work its way through the system, Shane received a settlement for ten percent of the three-million-dollar lawsuit, leaving him with two hundred thousand dollars after his lawyer's third was removed just weeks after turning twenty-two.

All of this of course is yet to come, as we currently await Detective Tommy Keane to awaken to a new day, and a new case, which may become another chapter in his story.

Read on for a sneak peek at the next book in the Tommy Keane series:

Rory O'Carroll

10:44 AM 1607 2nd Avenue

Clay pulled into the bus stop and parked the car a few buildings up from the Ballymurphy Pub, where three patrol cars were parked outside, and uniformed officers were stationed in front of.

The four of them exited their vehicle and approached the bar, nodding to the uniformed officers as they did. The front door to the bar was propped open with a trash can, something Sergeant Rotanelli, a short, stocky woman with salt and pepper hair and eighteen years on the job, who stood just inside the entrance like a Pitbull waiting for the squad to arrive, had done to keep people from continually touching the door before it had been checked for fingerprints and/or DNA.

Tommy was the first to step inside.

"Detective Keane," said Sergeant Rotanelli, greeting him as he did, "Is this going to be your case, Detective?"

"Yeah, Sarge, it is. What do you got for us?"

Sergeant Rotanelli turned and, raising her hand, pointing down the length of the bar, began, "Got one vic, name of Rory O'Carroll, he's the owner operator of the establishment, and is lying face down behind the bar over there. This gentleman here is Michael McDermott; he is the man who found O'Carroll behind the bar. I didn't get too close, and I haven't touched anything, and supposedly neither have Officers Wright or Donalds, who were first on the scene either. It appears to me our vic, O'Carroll, was shot in the head."

Rotanelli paused for a moment, then continued, "Both Wright and Donalds cleared the bar, bathrooms, kitchen, and basement, finding no one here other than Mr. McDermott, who made the call to 911 on the premises. The Medical Examiner and Crime Scene have been notified… And I think that's all I have for you at the moment, Detective."

"Thanks, Sarge. Who propped open the door with the trash can?"

"I did, didn't want everyone touching the door and ruining any prints or evidence."

"Good move, thank you." Tommy stepped past her and slowly made his way down the bar, taking in as much as he could as he did. It was an older establishment, and it looked it. Still, it was kept very clean, and its age added to its character. Tommy took in the smell, that old bar smell of stale beer and stories.

Tommy loved a quiet, empty bar in the morning and had frequented the Ballymurphy several times over the years, as well as the Old Gallway Home, which inhabited the same space for decades before O'Carroll had purchased it some twenty-five years ago. Even though he didn't know
Rory O'Carroll personally, he was quite familiar with
the bar itself.

Mark and Clay both followed slowly, also just taking in everything they could from the scene. Doreen stopped and spoke briefly with Sergeant Rotanelli before continuing down the length of the bar to join Mark and Clay as Tommy made his way around the bar and stood over the body.

He squatted down, careful not to touch anything as he did, "Looks like two entry wounds, one in the back of the head, and one in his back, just under his left shoulder blade, no blood really, so he was probably killed instantly." He said aloud, both making his observation to himself and sharing it with the others.

Tommy stood over the body. To his right was one of two cash registers; the drawer was slightly open, and he could see change in the drawers' wells. Using a pen, he opened it further; it was fully stocked with cash for the day.

To the right of the cash register was a small flat-bottomed canvas bag. Using the pen, he maneuvered the opening of the bag to reveal what would end up being $500 in cash, $200 in singles, $200 in fives, and one hundred in quarters.

He then stepped past the body and made his way to the second register. He stared at the keys for a moment, then, again, using the pen he had in his hand, hit the N/S key (No Sale), and the drawer popped open; it was also full of cash.

"Two registers full of cash, and what appears to be a change bag full of money, I don't see anything out of place here, not a single bottle or glass misplaced or broken, all the barstools neat and orderly, our victims clothing doesn't appear to be messed up or disheveled in any way, fuck me his clothes are still perfectly pressed… I don't think we have a fight or a robbery here, nope, this was something else."

"A hit." Said Doreen.

"Yup, that's what it looks like to me," Tommy replied.

About the Authors

Travis Myers and Natasha Myers Marsiguerra are a brother and sister team who both grew up in New York City.

Travis is a retired New York City Police Detective, and Natasha works and lives in California.

Together, they form a perfect team in that Travis, who has more stories to tell than a pub full of Irishmen, suffers from dyslexia and abhors anything to do with reading or writing. Natasha, his beloved little sister, is an avid reader of absolutely anything that is put in front of her and has been blessed with the gift of gab. She can out-story just about anyone, in any room, at any given time, and she can also type 60 words per minute. More importantly, Natasha is able to understand where her older brother is coming from, and craft his stories into a readable format.

Together, they weave the Tommy Keane Detective series into well-braided fictional tales that are nearly all based on actual events that they, and their friends and relatives, have lived. Travis and Natasha deliver on their promise to tell gritty, honest stories that are rooted in the everyday lives of everyday people.